*A
Harlequin
Romance*

BLEAK HERITAGE

by

JEAN S. MACLEOD

HARLEQUIN **BOOKS**

Winnipeg • Canada   New York • New York

BLEAK HERITAGE

Originally published by Mills & Boon Limited,
50 Grafton Way, Fitzroy Square, London, England.

Harlequin Canadian edition published October, 1970
Harlequin U.S. edition published January, 1971

Standard Book Number: 373-51440-9.

Printed in Canada

CHAPTER ONE

RHONA MAILLAND turned at the bedroom door for one final look at her son tucked up safely for the night in the cot which stood in the corner between the window and the fireplace.

"Good-night, darling!" she whispered, waiting for the slow smile of recognition to cross the child's face, before she finally closed the door.

She stood for a moment outside, leaning back against the thin panelling, conscious of a great weariness at the end of this day, a weariness that was both physical and mental, for eight months is no great length of time in which to recover from the shock of a beloved husband's death six weeks after the birth of his child. It seemed to Rhona as she closed her eyes for a moment that she would never be able to shut out the memory of those hours after the telegram announcing Alan's death had shattered her world, hours when she had sat, stunned and helpless because there had been no one to turn to, no one who cared. Her own people were dead and Molly Lang had been on her honeymoon at the time.

But Molly was waiting for her now! She straightened and moved across the narrow hall of the bungalow to the dining-room door. It had been decided from experience that it was best not to let Molly follow up the frolic of bath time by an excursion to the bedroom since Robin Mailland, at nine months old, was already conscious that he could twist this desirable stranger round his chubby little finger.

Molly was folding Robin's bath towel when her friend entered, and she looked up with a smile.

"Well, all settled for the night?" she enquired, and then, at sight of Rhona's pale face she pulled an occasional chair up to the fire. "Now, come on, sit down for half an hour, Rho, and we'll idle and gossip a bit."

Rhona hesitated, knowing that the door behind her shut off a rather untidy kitchen.

"I should get these things done, Molly," she began.

"Half an hour won't make any difference to two cups and saucers and a couple of plates!" Molly interrupted firmly. "If you do have visitors you needn't show them into the kitchen!"

Rhona smiled as she gave way.

"No," she said, "I could even bring them in here, thanks to you! Do you never get tired of visiting me three nights a week and tidying up the aftermath of a baby's bath time?"

"The fun of the actual bathing is well worth it," Molly said lightly as she drew out her cigarette case and offered her friend a cigarette. "Now, relax!"

Rhona settled herself in the chair on the other side of the hearth with a little sigh.

"I'm too lazy even to powder my nose," she observed.

"Or too tired, Rho?"

Molly had leaned forward to ask the question, though she felt that it scarcely required an answer.

"I'll go to bed early," Rhona said without making a direct reply.

"You have a long, full day," Molly said, watching her thoughtfully. "I wish you could get some help in the house."

Without looking up Rhona replied quite frankly:

"Alan's pension wouldn't run to that. It's keeping us comfortably enough, but—no luxuries!"

Molly hesitated, and then she looked across the hearth with a determined light in her eyes.

"Look here, Rhona," she said, "don't think I'm butting in out of idle curiosity or anything like that—

I'm not. But—aren't the Maillands doing anything for you? After all," she went on in her blunt way, "you are Alan's wife and Robin is his son."

A look of pain passed in her friend's dark eyes.

"You know I wouldn't ask their help," she said with brief finality.

"I know. But I thought they might have offered it."

There was a silence and then Rhona said:

"You know they would never recognise me in the first place. Ours was such a whirlwind romance"—she smiled tenderly at her memories—"that it never seemed to occur to me that I hadn't met Alan's people till we were married and settled down here in Glasgow."

"And they refused point-blank to meet you afterwards?"

Rhona nodded.

"That's what made it so difficult to write to them last week about—about Alan's letter," she said slowly.

Molly remained silent, her rather large mouth firmly set, her eyes, which were placed too far apart in a broad face for any pretence at beauty, more thoughtful than ever.

"It's a problem," she said. "Though I suppose you couldn't do any other than write to them in face of that letter of Alan's."

"It was his last request," Rhona said softly, her eyes filling with sudden tears. "It was almost as if he feared that something would separate us and—and he wanted me to take his son to Kindarroch." She paused. "He said—that first time he saw Robin: 'So here you are at last—our son and the heir to Kindarroch!' He was so proud of the old place, Molly, and he could never quite believe that his family could hold out so long."

Molly Lang's eyes were blazing now.

7

"I'd like to meet old Mailland! It would give me the greatest pleasure to tell him what I thought of them for the way they have treated you!" she declared. "I wouldn't feel so strongly if they had met you and found you wanting, but to condemn you unseen——!"

Rhona bit her lip.

"That's what hurt most in the beginning," she confessed. "The fact that they wouldn't accept me because I had worked in a shop. It was what kept Alan away from Kindarroch—the injustice of it."

"The snobbishness of it!" Molly threw her cigarette into the fire, a fine scorn in her eyes. "What do you think their reply will be to your suggestion that you should bring Robin to Kindarroch?"

"I don't know." There was a trace of nervousness in Rhona's voice now. "I don't think I mind very much, Molly," she went on, "if they do refuse. I had to write to them because of that letter of Alan's— because he considered it his son's birthright, but if the Maillands refuse to accept us I am still quite able to support Robin—even if I have to work for him. I'm not afraid of work."

Molly Lang, seeing the fire in the dark eyes, knew it the reflection of an unquenchable spirit, a spirit tired though never beaten, and she wondered rather fearfully what the next few weeks would bring in their train. She had known about the last letter of Alan Mailland's for some time now, known that the decision it demanded had contributed largely to Rhona's heartache.

"Well," she said aloud, "I suppose they *will* answer your letter? In case not, have you made any other plans?"

"Plans? No—no, I haven't thought of anything else. You see, since I read Alan's letter all those months ago I've always accepted the thought that I would go to Kindarroch sooner or later. I've got to try," Rhona added slowly, "to see things from their point of view, Molly—family inheritance, the continuation of their name through the male line and all that sort of thing. It's important to them."

"Yes," Molly said slowly, "I suppose it is important to them." She rose and stirred the coals to a blaze with a little vicious movement which seemed to afford her some measure of relief. "All the same, don't let them trample on you, Rhona. I'm sorry I'm going away to-morrow, but you know how it is. I'll be back, though, before you go off to the ancestral home!" she added lightly.

"I'm glad this isn't good-bye," Rhona said as she followed her friend into the little kitchenette of the home which she knew she would leave with a heavy heart. "What time are you going to-morrow?"

"Early. The eight-fifteen from Central," Molly said, and fell easily into talk of her nursing job.

She referred to the subject of Kindarroch again just before she left.

"If you had even seen any of the Maillands I would feel easier in my mind about the whole affair," she said, "but as it is it's like walking into a den of strange animals and announcing that you've come to share their dinner. They may tear you apart."

"I've seen a photograph of Alan's mother," Rhona said with a little smile twitching the corners of her mouth. "She looks much too proud to stoop to tearing anyone apart."

"I can imagine the type," Molly returned, and then, her arm round her friend's slim shoulders: "Don't let anything I've said discourage you, Rho! Once they've met you they'll change their mind, and always remember that you're doing this for Robin—not for the sake of their wretched pride. It will bring you a lot of comfort in time. She slipped into the coat her friend held out for her, gathering up handbag and gloves from the hallstand. "May I peep at the scamp before I go?" she asked. "I'll be very quiet!"

"He won't wake."

Rhona stood at the door while her friend tiptoed softly across the bedroom and bent swiftly to drop a light kiss on her son's unconscious brow.

"I'll write as soon as ever I get a definite enough address," Molly assured her as they went down the narrow pathway to the gate together, "so don't worry if you don't hear from me for a couple of weeks. And—keep your chin up!"

"I'll be waiting eagerly for your first letter," Rhona told her, "and I'll send back all the news in mine."

"Even if it's from Kindarroch?"

"Even from Kindarroch—or half-way across the world!"

Rhona stood watching Molly's departing figure until it was swallowed up in the grey dusk, and then she turned back into the bungalow and closed the door securely behind her. At first she had thought that it would be impossible to live alone like this after Alan had gone, but, strangely enough, the very fact of being responsible for the tiny life in the cot through there in the bedroom had dispersed her fears and given her a quiet courage to carry on even after the crushing blow of her husband's death.

To-night, however, she found it impossible to settle to the task of mending which she had assigned herself and, reaching up, she switched off the lamp and sat in the flickering shadows of firelight and gave herself up to thoughts of the future.

Robin was already in his pram in the autumn sunshine which flooded over the front garden when the postman brought two letters to No. 17 Balgray Avenue.

Rhona, seeing him from the window of the front bedroom where she was making the bed, dropped the padded silk coverlet on the nearest chair and ran out to the hall. The door was lying open and the postman had left her small mail on the mat. She stooped to pick it up with bated breath and the colour rising in a swift wave to her pale cheeks.

The first letter was typewritten, one of these psuedo-personal advertisements which had become common of late, so she turned to the second envelope for what she sought, finding her name written across it in bold, upright characters in a woman's hand with the Calendar postmark visible above the stamp.

So, it had come! Sooner than she had expected, really, she thought, as, with a glance at her sleeping son, she carried the missive which would decide his future into the dining-room and slit the flap with nervous fingers.

A single sheet of thick notepaper was the total content and, glancing quickly to the foot of the page, she saw the brief signature: "Sincerely, CATHERINE MAILLAND."

Alan's mother! Rhona's heart began to beat madly as she turned back to the top of the page and read the short note through to the end. Gradually a look of disappointment crept into her eyes and the excited flush faded from her cheeks. The letter from which she had expected so much told her so little. Couched in the most formal terms, it remarked that Mrs. Mailland had been 'surprised and interested' to receive her daughter-in-law's communication and, after consultation with the remaining members of the family, had decided, in the interests of the continuation of the male line of succession at Kindarroch, to accept Alan's suggestion that his son should be brought up there.

"I was about to make a similar suggestion myself," wrote Catherine Mailland towards the end of her brief note, "and had already mentioned the matter to our solicitor, in whose hands I propose to leave all arrangements in the future. You will, therefore, be receiving a visit from Mr. Murray one day next week and I sincerely hope that we can bring about a suitable arrangement.

"Sincerely,
"CATHERINE MAILLAND."

Rhona re-read this strange missive with a little quiver of distress added to her first disappointment. She had prepared herself for many things, but not quite this—not the cold formality of her mother-in-law's brief, almost businesslike communication. And the mention of the solicitor? Was it strictly necessary to put their transfer to Kindarroch on such a formal footing? Surely there could be nothing to concern a solicitor in the simple fact of her going to Kindarroch with her child to live with her husband's people? Perhaps, she thought rather wearily as she stood staring down at the letter and trying to read into it a kindliness that was not there, it had something to do with the succession. She wasn't very well versed in such matters, but surely that could have waited until they were settled in and had got to know each other a little.

Going about her morning tasks, she found herself touching simple household goods tenderly, lingering wistfully over the dusting of the piano where she and Alan had spent many happy hours, passing from room to room in her tiny castle with a growing sense of ineffable loss. It was her home and she was leaving it, and perhaps she was shedding with it all the happiness it had held for her, a happiness which still lingered there in spite of the sorrow she had known within the cramped space of its four beloved walls.

The thought of the letter she had received from Kindarroch kept recurring to her troubled mind, phrases from it jumping out at her almost mockingly. 'After consultation with the remaining members of the family,' Mrs. Mailland had decided to write! The remaining members of the family, as far as Rhona knew, consisted of Alan's father and his sister, Gertrude, who was four years his senior. Hector Mailland had held his son's respect and affection even after the family's refusal to accept his wife, but Alan had rarely mentioned his mother and had dismissed Gertrude with the remark that she had the makings of a disgruntled old maid.

Rhona, in the first flush of her married happiness, had not been unduly curious about the in-laws who obviously considered a shop assistant in a big Glasgow store a very unfitting match for the heir to Kindarroch and the name of Mailland, and she wondered now rather bitterly if they would consider her son in the same light, accepting him only because they had no other choice.

As the days passed, however, and she tried to accustom herself to the thought of the drastic change all this would make in her life, she began to feel a little warmer towards the Maillands. After all, they were Alan's people and she may be judging them harshly. They may even be trying, in their willingness to accept Robin and her at Kindarroch, to make amends for their injustice in the past.

The small comfort of this thought was quickly driven out by the reflection that it was eight months since Alan had died in a French hospital and in all that time she had not received one word of sympathy from his people. It was almost as if they had decided that she did not exist at all until they had discovered that Alan had left a son—and an heir to Kindarroch.

At the beginning of the following week she received a letter from a firm of solicitors in Edinburgh whose name seemed strangely familiar to her, to say that their Mr. Murray would call upon her on the Wednesday of that week to discuss the business mentioned in Mrs. Mailland's letter. The name Murray, Fengrove and Murray kept recurring to her as she dressed Robin for his afternoon walk, but it was not until she was well along the wide stretch of the Kilmarnock Road, revelling in the clean breath of the wind from the open moor, that she remembered the connection.

It all came back to her with a little rush. It had happened about a week after their marriage when they were still in Edinburgh on their short honeymoon and Alan had said quite casually one morning:

"I'm going up to see an old friend. He's a solicitor. I want you to come with me, Rhona."

She had hesitated, feeling shy about meeting any of his former friends, for in spite of her brave determination to ignore it, the attitude of his family towards her had carried its sting. Alan had had his way, however, and they had ascended to the offices of Murray, Fengrove and Murray and had met Mr. Murray who had talked to them kindly in a fatherly way that had warmed Rhona's heart. Robert Murray had shown no outward surprise when Alan had ended the personal flow of conversation by coming to business and refusing with the utmost finality to touch a penny of the allowance which his family had decided that it was their duty to make to him. His young face had been hard and unyielding and the old lawyer had not pressed the point, but Rhona had always thought of him kindly afterwards because he had said, as he had held her hand at parting:

"Some day I am going to come and see you in that bungalow at Giffnock, Mrs. Mailland. Until then, God bless you, my dear!"

And now he was coming! So long afterwards, Rhona thought, and then realised that it was not so long when just measured by actual time. It was because she had lived through so much in those two brief years that made that last day of her honeymoon seem so far away, lost in the haze of bitter-sweet memory.

It was, therefore, with a feeling of anticipation that she rose earlier than usual on the Wednesday morning and hurried through her work, dressing Robin and putting him out in the sun to kick his sturdy little legs to his heart's content.

Her mind flew off to other things. What sort of sandwiches to make for the cup of afternoon tea she had decided to offer the old solicitor on his arrival; whether Mabel Rush from the bungalow on the corner of Balgray Avenue would come along in plenty of time to take Robin out for his afternoon walk before Mr. Murray arrived; whether Robin would be safe and well-behaved with the Rush family until bath time and, finally, whether she had done right in accepting Mrs. Rush's offer when she had never allowed anyone to wheel Robin out before.

Mabel Rush arrived shortly after the clock on the dining-room mantelpiece had struck two.

"I'll take good care of him, Mrs. Mailland," Mabel said. "Don't worry about us at all. I'll go down to the park where there's no traffic."

Suddenly Rhona knew that she would not worry, but she said, all the same:

"I think you should bring him back at half-past four, Mabel. Mr. Murray might want to see him."

Mabel went off proudly. Apart from her devotion to Robin, it was something to be said for her trustworthyness that Mrs. Mailland had agreed to let her wheel him out. Mabel, who was just sixteen, adored babies and had decided to become a nurse at the Children's Hospital.

Rhona ran through to the bedroom and watched the progress of the navy-blue pram down the Avenue until it had passed out of sight behind the last bungalow before she turned to the wardrobe and took out her solitary afternoon dress, a simple little lavender crepe which suited her dark colouring admirably. Its simple lines moulded her slim figure with subtle flattery, for it had been purchased at the shop in Sauchiehall Street where she had been head saleswoman in the gown department and where the buyer had told her—in a rare, expansive moment— that she had a flair for clothes and knew how to wear them to advantage.

It was not this flair for clothes that she was thinking of at the moment, however, as she slipped last year's model over her head, but the old gentleman with the kind eyes and friendly manner who had shaken her by the hand and wished her God-speed two years ago in Edinburgh.

How glad she was that he should come to her first! She even felt that she might be able to ask him about the Maillands—about the things she should know in order to create that first good impression which she was determined to achieve. She wouldn't need to ask him about Kindarroch, she reflected, for she felt that she knew all about the place already. Alan had spoken about his home so often; sometimes in unguarded moments his tone had been wistful and it was the memory of this fact that had helped to sway her decision to carry out his wish.

Well, at least, she would not be nervous of meeting Mr. Murray——

The bell rang and the familiar summons sent her heart racing wildly. With a last hurried glance in the mirror to smooth her hair, she went into the hall and opened the door.

"Oh——!"

The exclamation was entirely involuntary and her excitement turned to confusion as she wondered what chance had sent another visitor to her door on this important afternoon.

"Mrs. Mailland?"

"Yes." She thought that his voice matched the fine, direct look of his grey eyes. "I'm afraid," she apologised, "that I am at a loss——"

He smiled, a smile that lit up his eyes and erased lines which looked like the marks of pain from the corners of his firm mouth.

"My name is Murray—Neil Murray." As he changed his stick from his right hand to the left and felt in an inside pocket she saw that he had been leaning heavily on that stick and immediately stood aside.

"Please come in," she invited.

"I should have had my card ready," he said, "especially since I am here in my father's stead, but I'm afraid two years in the Air Force obliterates business details to some extent!"

Nervously she preceded him into the drawing-room and indicated the arm-chair where she had pictured the elderly solicitor sitting down to face her across the hearth.

"Perhaps we had better come to business right away," Neil Murray began, producing a foolscap envelope from his breast pocket, yet he sat with it between his hands for many minutes before he spoke again, as if the task which faced him had suddenly become the most uncongenial one in the world.

Rhona was aware that he was scrutinising her closely and that surprise and a suggestion of embarrassment were in his clear grey eyes.

"Mrs. Hector Mailland had asked my firm to act for her in this matter, Mrs. Mailland," he said. "She has written to you, of course, acquainting you with the fact that she is willing to accept her grandson at Kindarroch."

"Yes," she said quickly, feeling as if a strong hand had gripped her by the throat. "I wrote explaining that Alan—my husband wanted us to go there."

He glanced up at her, frank pity in his eyes.

"And Mrs. Mailland made it quite plain, of course, that she is only willing to accept your son?"

Rhona half rose in her chair.

"What do you mean?" she whispered.

"I'm afraid," he said tensely, "that Mrs. Mailland cannot understand why you should feel that you—will be necessary at Kindarroch."

"But she can't do that!" she cried, her cheeks aflame, a sudden burning sense of injustice throbbing within her. "She can't take Robin from me!"

"No," he returned slowly, "you would have to agree to let your son go."

She stared at him.

"Agree to let him go?" A queer little mirthless smile hovered at the corners of her mouth for a moment. "But surely they don't understand what they're asking. Surely they don't realise how much —how much he means to me?"

She was looking at her visitor now almost beseechingly as if, in convincing this stranger with the deep-set grey eyes and the kind mouth, she might be able to convince the Maillands at whose bidding he had come.

"Of course," he said rather awkwardly, looking away from the unconscious appeal in her eyes, "Mrs. Mailland realises that, but she seemed to think that the boy's place was at Kindarroch, that he would have a better chance in life if he was brought up there——"

"Away from my influence!" Rhona flashed, a sudden gust of anger sweeping aside the first stunned

18

feeling of helplessness. "I can work for my son, Mr. Murray. I am young and strong and he will not starve!"

He looked at her, a hint of admiration in his grave eyes, yet he felt compelled to say:

"Would it be quite the same? Forgive me putting it this way to you, Mrs. Mailland, but I'm sure Alan envisaged the very best for his son—life as he had known it, and—probably at Kindarroch."

All the anger died out of Rhona Mailland's face at his words and she had to grip the arms of her chair to hide the sudden trembling of her hands as the memory of her husband's letter swept across her mind and she realised that this had been his last wish. His son at Kindarroch! He had wanted that, but how could she bear to part with Robin? The Maillands did not know what they were asking. Any sacrifice rather than this!

"What am I to do?" she said. "I can't part with my baby—I can't give him up, yet—yet I know it was Alan's wish and I suppose—I suppose it would be best for him in the end in a material sense." She rose to her feet, her eyes filled with sudden, hopeless tears. "Oh, why had they to do this! Why couldn't they have accepted me for just a time? It's so cruel—so senseless to judge people untried. I would have done my best—for Alan's sake." She turned away to the window, fighting for the self-control which had slipped from her in this supreme moment of anguish. "I suppose," she said slowly at last, "there isn't the slightest chance of them changing their minds about me?"

"I'm afraid not." His voice still held that note of profound sympathy. "In the interview I had with your mother-in-law before I left Kindarroch she made it quite clear that there was to be no way round the bargain."

"And my father-in-law—Mr. Mailland?" Rhona asked without quite knowing why.

"I don't think Mr. Mailland had much to say in the matter," he replied, adding quickly: "Of course, he's ready and willing to welcome your son."

Alan's son! Rhona thought bitterly, and the whole dreadful, sickening feeling of acute misery overwhelmed her anew. What was she to do? But was there any question of what she was to do? Rebelliously she told herself that she would not give up her child—rather let them both starve together first!—and then the crushing certainty of her dead husband's wish presented itself again and she felt suddenly incapable of decision.

"Mrs. Mailland has made every provision for your son," Neil Murray was saying. "She has made enquiries at one of the best training establishments in Edinburgh for a certified nurse so that you need not fear that he will not be properly cared for."

"A nurse!" Rhona repeated tensely, her hands clenched suddenly by her side. "Oh, yes, all that money can buy! but will money compensate for what they are taking away? Have they thought of that?"

"Your boy is very young, Mrs. Mailland."

"All the more reason why he needs me! Oh, can't you see—can't *you* understand, at least?"

All the hardness of anger had gone out of her and she stood before him, a curiously beaten look in her dark eyes, so that suddenly a wild desire rose within Neil Murray to advise her to keep her child and let his future look after itself.

"Do you think," Rhona said slowly, her tortured mind grasping at the meagre straws of hope, "that if I—did agree to let him go I could see him sometimes? Would—Alan's mother agree to that?"

"It would not be often," he said. "Mrs. Mailland expressed the opinion that a clean break would be the best way for the child."

"I see." Rhona's face was deadly pale now. "They won't even give me half a chance."

Her voice quivered on the last words and her teeth bit into her lower lip in a nervous attempt to steady it. A terrible feeling of being remote from the whole world took possession of her so that she seemed to be wandering in a barren plain of desperate indecision with no friendly hand stretched out to guide her. What was she to do? To whom was she to turn?

Suddenly, out of the mist of pain that seemed to have enveloped her for an endless age, a man's face took shape and she looked across her own hearth and saw kindliness and sympathy reflected in a man's clear, grey eyes.

"Oh, Mr. Murray," she appealed, "help me to make this decision. What would you do?"

Neil Murray's eyes fell before the direct look in hers; he who had always met men's eyes squarely, who had faced grave issues unflinchingly, looked away from the pleading in a woman's eyes because he felt himself in duty bound to a client and an old friend to answer:

"I would let him go."

Rhona recoiled before the words, drawing in a long, quivering breath. What had she expected? Hope had gone with his answer, but it had given birth to doubt in her mind, doubt of her right to stand in her son's way, doubt of her right to disregard her husband's expressed wish.

And so she answered him at last, slowly almost tonelessly:

"Very well. You can tell—them that I'll let Robin go."

Neil Murray stood at the window for several seconds longer gazing out at the little strip of carefully tended garden, wondering about little things that seemed of no great consequence. How this girl managed to care for the miniature plot; how she had time to do the housework and look after her child and yet tend to the garden too, and saw in it all a reflection of a brave character that had risen above sorrow and frustration and deadly despair to meet life nobly, to carry on with the little things of everyday existence, presenting a brave face to the world, as if love and grief and pain had never been her lot. Only in her dark eyes lay the poignant shadow of their reflection. It seemed inconceivable to him at that moment that it should have fallen to his lot to deal her this final deadly blow.

Suddenly he turned, the desire strong in him to unsay his last decisive words, but already he saw the effect of them mirrored in her eyes. She seemed to have summoned all her resources—pride, a gentle dignity, even kindness—to meet him.

"You have been very good—bearing with me like this," she said, and somehow the very flatness of her tone told him that her decision was made and that not even a complete reversal of his former opinion could change it.

She had, he thought, accepted something which she considered inevitable.

"If you will tell me what I must do," she said haltingly. "Is there—anything to sign?"

"There's nothing more we can do at present." He felt a desire to get out into the fresh air as quickly as possible, to get away from the slowly growing idea that he had inflicted a desperate wrong upon this brave creature. "Mrs. Mailland will send the nurse for the little boy and I suppose she will write to you again before then, making all the necessary arrangements."

He hesitated, wondering what more to say. She seemed to have forgotten him as she stood there gazing unseeingly at the clock ticking so unconcernedly away on the mantelpiece before her. *Was* there anything more to say? He had carried out his instructions, completed his part of the ghastly business, yet he still stood there waiting, feeling that there was something more to say.

Then, suddenly, he said it—against all his training, against all professional etiquette, advice she had not asked for, given on impulse right from the bottom of an essentially generous heart.

"Don't let them take your son completely, Mrs. Mailland. Insist on seeing him occasionally if you wish it, and—don't sign anything."

He was gone almost before Rhona had realised it, and she was standing at the window looking after his tall figure as he limped slowly along the pavement and, turning into Farnham Drive, was finally lost to view.

A thousand times during the days which followed Rhona regretted her decision and yet, almost as strong as her regret, was the conviction that what she was about to do would be best for her son in the future.

At the end of the week the expected letter arrived from her mother-in-law and to Rhona, because of the concession it conferred, it appeared less cruel than Catherine Mailland's former missive. Mrs. Mailland wrote that she was quite willing to agree to her daughter-in-law seeing Robin once a year in Edinburgh at the offices of the family solicitor and that the child might spend the day with her provided that it was understood that he should not know who she was. That, Mrs. Hector Mailland felt, would merely tend to confuse his young mind. And to this cruel and heartless concession Rhona Mailland clung as to a ray of hope, reading into it far more kindliness than was ever intended and blinding herself completely to other issues involved because she was to be permitted one yearly glimpse of her son. To her torn heart at that moment the joy of the thought eclipsed all else and it seemed as much as she had dared to hope for. One day out of a year! Could she—would they grant her his birthday?

Her mother-in-law's letter was intended as a final communication from Kindarroch. All other matters, Mrs. Mailland wrote, would be settled in future through the solicitors. She had arranged for a nurse for the child who would call at Giffnock and take him to Kindarroch. It was made quite plain that Rhona's presence, even to take her child to his new home, was not desirable.

"I couldn't take him, anyway," she whispered aloud as she read that final callous paragraph. "I couldn't bear to come away—alone."

It was in this frame of mind that Molly Lang found her on the Thursday afternoon when she returned to Glasgow unexpectedly and came straight out to the bungalow for tea, sure of her welcome. Rhona had written of her decision, explaining the circumstances as best she could, and though Molly was not at all sure that she had taken the right step, she felt that Rhona's decision had been sealed by some important conviction and that she would not change her mind now. To utter her own doubts would only cause her friend added heartache, she decided, and so she sat listening to Rhona's further explanations, tight-lipped and curiously silent.

"And when," she asked at last, "does this merciless transaction come into force?"

"To-morrow. The nurse is coming for him to-morrow."

Molly looked up sharply.

"So soon? They're not giving you much time."

Rhona gave a little involuntary shiver.

"Does it matter?" she asked. "It would only be time to regret."

Why not throw the whole ghastly business up right now? Molly was tempted to ask, but refrained

because she felt that she had no real right to interfere.

"Rhona," she said, "when is this woman coming
—the nurse, I mean?"

"At three o'clock. I—I've a feeling she will be
here prompt."

Molly bit her lip. Poor Rhona! Counting the
minutes now!

"Look here," she said briskly, to stem her own
emotion, "let me see to this for you, Rho. You'll
never do it yourself. It's—just not humanly possible,
I guess. I know I couldn't if I were in your place.
Go out somewhere, Rho—into the park or up to
Mrs. Rush and I'll wait here for the nurse."

"Oh, Molly!" Rhona buried her face in her
hands, her voice coming through them in a smothered
whisper. "What a coward I am after making such a
decision, but I feel that I can't part with him like
that—just handing him over to a stranger—a woman
I have never seen before."

"Do you think it would be easier leaving him with
me?" Molly asked huskily.

"Yes—a little easier."

"Then, we'll do it that way," Molly declared.

And so, on the following afternoon when Robin
Mailland woke from his after-dinner nap his mother
lifted him from his pram for the last time and carried
him into the bungalow where his white woollen coat
and leggings lay ready on the table and his clothes
were packed in the blue suit-case which Rhona had
bought for her honeymoon.

Her hands trembled as she dressed him with meti-
culous care, lingering over tiny buttons caressingly
until Molly, who stood watching dumbly, had to
turn away.

In the end Rhona sat him in his pram again and
kissed him and went hatless into the autumn sunshine, walking like a creature in a dream, her heart

empty, her lip caught between her teeth. She walked on stumblingly across tram lines and over busy crossings until at last she found herself in the sequestered walks of Rouken Glen where she had come so often with the pram that even now she could scarcely believe that she was not pushing it before her.

The empty feeling of her hands rushed in upon her as she went slowly along a favourite path leading to the waterfall and she sank down on a nearby bench and sat staring into space, recalling all the happiness of the past nine months apart from their sorrow, a happiness that her son alone had made possible. The first time he had sat up she had brought him here and he had gazed at the water cascading over the stones with big, wondering eyes and made tiny gurgling noises to it, laughing at the spray falling down in a gentle shower while she had pretended to catch it for him, laughing, too—laughter that had helped to ease the pain at her heart.

Now that pain was a deadly, empty ache stretching down into the future. If only she had never listened to advice, no matter how kindly offered! If only Alan had not made that last request——!

Suddenly, she was on her feet and running back along the way she had come. She could not—*would* not give him up like this! Her breath was coming in tiny gasps as she turned out of the gates and along the pavement as if some monstrous horde was pressing at her heels.

Nearing home, she crossed Eastwood Toll against the traffic lights and began to run again, yet her feet seemed again weighted, as in some dreadful nightmare. Turning at the top of Farnham Drive, she looked down the length of the Avenue and her legs suddenly refused to carry her a step further.

Half-way down the Avenue a taxi was moving away from the green gate of the bungalow, and Molly

Lang was standing with her back to the gate as if she, too, could not bear to see it go.

"I've got to find something to do, Molly."

Rhona sat with the *Herald* unopened before her as if, having made the statement, she had not even the courage to open the newspaper. It was a month since that dreadful day of Robin's departure, and every day had served only to increase her loneliness and add to her heartache. True, Molly had stayed with her, and she knew that she would never have got through those first agonising days but for her friend.

"Give it a trial," Molly had advised, "now that you have taken the plunge," but she knew that, deep in the secret places of her friend's heart, regret gnawed ceaselessly.

"What do you fancy doing?" Molly asked now. "Will you go back into shop work?"

Rhona nodded.

"I suppose so."

She sat for a moment or two longer gazing into space, her coffee untouched, and then she unfolded the newspaper and glanced at the column of situations vacant.

Molly watched her, perturbed at the pallor of her face and the droop of her sensitive mouth, and then, suddenly, Rhona's half-hearted scrutiny changed to one of deep and excited interest.

"Molly," she breathed at last, "look here!"

Molly put her napkin down on her plate, and went round behind her friend's chair, reading the small paragraph under Rhona's trembling finger.

"WANTED [it ran] "an under-nurse for child eleven months old. Apply direct to Kindarroch, Perthshire, enclosing references and recent photograph."

"Molly," Rhona said slowly, "I'm going to apply for that job."

"But," Molly objected, hating herself even as she did so, "how can you possibly, Rho? You see," she added weakly, looking away from the dark eyes where sudden hope was dying, "they are asking for references."

Rhona's shoulders hunched forward.

"Yes—I see." She sat staring down at the printed page until it swam in a grey blur before her eyes, and then, suddenly, her head went back and the light of desperate resolution shone on her face. "I don't care," she declared passionately, "I mean to have that job, Molly—even if I have to forge a dozen references to get it!"

In the silence which followed her impassioned words, Molly stood very still.

"You won't have to forge even one reference," she said slowly at last, "because, you see, you are going to borrow mine."

Rhona looked up, amazed.

"Yours? But, Molly, I couldn't do that. There might be trouble. You'd be running a risk if—if we were ever discovered."

"Not any greater risk than you would run with your ridiculous forged references," her friend declared firmly. She had the situation in hand now, and the help she could afford Rhona seemed nothing short of an act of Providence. References lying idle, and Rhona Mailland in need of references, in such great need of them that she had been ready to stoop to a minor crime to obtain them! "Yes," she continued deliberately, "you must use mine. Nothing could be more simple, really. It works out every way. You can't go to Kindarroch as Rhona Mailland, that's agreed, isn't it? Well then, you must change your name, and Mary Grant's a perfectly good name so,

28

since I'm finished with it, I'm quite willing that you should use it—together with the references."

Rhona's eyes were alive now, shining like an eager child's, yet she still objected.

"I can't involve you——"

Molly perched herself on the edge of the table in a familiar attitude which spelled argument.

"Look here," she began, "there's to be no thought of me in this. I'm not going to stand by and see you forge references that would probably be detected as false at a first glance. If you mean to get to Kindarroch——"

"I *do* mean to, Molly!"

"Then you must have the correct background, and my references will provide you with just that. You didn't *ask* me for them, Rho. I made the offer."

Rhona looked up at her with a quivering smile.

"I can't understand why you are so—so good to me," she said haltingly.

"Can't you?" Molly smiled. "It's very simple!"

"Of course," Rhona said after a pause, her eyes darkening with sudden fear, "I may not get the job."

"You may not," Molly hesitated, studying her fingertips with a deep frown. "All the same," she ended at last, "I've a feeling—almost a premonition that you will!"

"Oh, if only I could!" The light in Rhona's eyes stirred her friend to the very depths of her being so that any fragment of doubt as to the advisability of the step she had taken was swept completely aside. "I've been living in absolute torture these past few weeks and now—now I know that I can't go on without Robin. He was part of me—all I had to live for."

"I know." Molly slipped off the table and put a kindly arm round the slim, silk-clad shoulders. "Well, that's settled," she declared in a lighter tone but with great determination. "I'll pop home and look out my refs., and you have a hunt round for your most presentable photograph." She paused half-way to the door. "You're quite sure the Maillands have never seen you before?"

"Absolutely certain."

"That makes it much easier. I'm warming to the plot already!" Molly grinned, determined to present their adventure in lighter vein if possible. "I believe I'm going to enjoy my part in it. I've always wanted to get one back at old Mailland!"

Rhona paled suddenly.

"Is it a—terribly mean trick, Molly?"

"Not one bit of it!" Molly turned with her hand on the door-knob. "What better nurse could Robin Mailland have than his own mother? You're not going to cheat them as far as willing service goes, are you?"

"No. No, I suppose not."

Rhona sat gazing into space long after her friend had gone, the newspaper still spread out on the table before her, the thoughts within her tumbling on like a swift-flowing stream. No, she would not be cheating the Maillands as far as eager service went, for what more loving care could Robin have than hers? Yet, she was going to Kindarroch against all their wishes. Well, they would not know! The determination within her to see her child, the magnet power of mother-love, was stronger than all her scruples. She would give them good and honest service. What more could they ask?

CHAPTER TWO

"I wish to heaven they'd make up their minds!"

Molly threw the end of her cigarette into the fire as she rose from the breakfast-table in her own bungalow a week later. The strained look on Rhona's face was becoming fixed now, and a hint of hopelessness was creeping into the dark eyes. It had been necessary to move to Molly's bungalow so that the address from which Rhona made her application would convey nothing to the Maillands, and Molly had felt that the change of scene would be a good thing for her friend in the meantime.

"I think they must have fixed on—someone else," Rhona said listlessly.

Molly began to collect the plates.

"The post hasn't come yet," she observed more cheerfully than she felt. "There may be a reply this morning."

Rhona did not answer. She sat still in her seat with her back to the fire as if all initiative, even to perform the routine tasks of life, had gone from her. Molly turned away to the kitchen with troubled eyes. She, also, had begun to lose hope, though not for one moment would she permit Rhona to suspect the fact. Then, suddenly, as she ran the hot-water tap the front door bell pealed, and there was a familiar rattling at the letter-box. Her heartbeats quickened to a mad race as she went swiftly through to the hall, but Rhona was there before her. Her face, which had been pale and pinched looking for days, was flushed, her eyes hungrily alight as she lifted the solitary envelope.

"It's from Kindarroch," she breathed, looking at the postmark. "Open it, Molly," she implored, "for I feel as if I couldn't."

Molly took the envelope and carried it back into the living-room before she attempted to open it. She read slowly, her face remaining gravely attentive until she reached the end.

"You're to go," she said, and she was glad that the sudden flatness of her voice was obliterated in Rhona's joyous cry.

"Oh—oh! I can't believe it!"

31

Molly smiled, knowing suddenly that she did so to cover the awakening of a new uneasiness, a feeling almost akin to fear, that gripped her throat like a strangling hand for a moment before she banished it to the background of her mind to make way for the reflection of her friend's overwhelming joy.

"I'm so glad it came before you had to go," Rhona said presently, a sentiment which Molly repeated often in her innermost heart during the three days which followed, days of whirlwind preparation, of cautions and planning, of selecting a suit and plain, sensible working frocks and overalls, of advice sought and offered freely and, finally, of hurried good-byes.

Molly travelled south to her hospital by a train twenty minutes after she had seen Rhona's steam out of Queen Street, and when she had finally settled in her corner she took time to wonder if, after all, they had done a completely wise thing.

Rhona, on the other hand, was too absorbed by the thought of seeing her son again to worry about the wisdom or otherwise of her action.

She changed at Stirling and, as the train wound into the wooded heart of Perthshire and giant hills rose up against the sky, she took out the formally worded letter which she had received three days ago and read it through again. She was going to Kindarroch on a month's trial, and at the end of that time Mrs. Hector Mailland would consider retaining her service until further notice.

She looked out of the window, seeing trees and hills in a shadowy haze and seeing through them a baby's face.

The train slid to a standstill and seemed to wait expectantly. A voice far down the narrow wooden platform shouted "Kin-darroch Junction", and Rhona roused herself from her day-dream, and wrenched open the carriage door, collecting her few belongings as the porter came up.

"You for Kindarroch House, Miss?" he asked familiarly. "You'll be the new nurse they're expectin'?"

Before she could reply he had lifted her small case and was walking across to a gate in the wooden fence.

"The car's come down for you," he intimated, as if it was all something quite personal.

A big saloon car was standing on the gravel of the incline, and a middle-aged man in uniform touched his cap as he came forward and relieved the porter of Rhona's case.

"This way, Miss." He smiled down at her. "I hope you've had a comfortable journey."

"Yes, thank you."

Rhona found herself installed in the back of the roomy car with her case on the seat beside the chauffeur, and for the first time a feeling of acute nervousness overwhelmed her and she was infinitely glad that she was alone and had a few minutes, at least, in which to fight this dread feeling. She realised that she must be completely mistress of herself before she reached Kindarroch as everything would depend upon the way she carried off that first vital interview with Alan's mother.

Glancing out of the window, she saw that the trees were thinning now and caught a gleam of grey water above which hills shouldered each other to the sky. A wind was bending the pines before it, and big white clouds scudded high above them like white-rigged ships sailing across the sun and sweeping light and shade over the distant glens which opened out at the head of Loch Darroch. She knew that she was near her destination, and sat forward to look more closely. The chauffeur turned in his seat.

"You'll see the house in a minute," he told her.

"Just a glimpse of it at that break in the trees yonder."

She waited, breathless. Her heart seemed to be beating a mad tattoo against her breast as she strained her eyes to catch a first glimpse of the house that now sheltered her son.

The car slowed down at the break in the trees which the chauffeur had indicated, and she saw the loch stretching out before her to the far hills and saw, on a grey promontory almost at their feet, the weather-beaten pile of Kindarroch standing against its grey background of foam-flecked water. It presented a cold, austere picture to her eager eyes, and something turned over in her breast.

It was the day, she thought, as the car swept on and her view of the house was obscured by trees once more. When the sun flashed out it must look different, less—sinister. Was that the word?

The sun did come out as they wound downhill to the level of the loch, and turned in between two iron gates along a short, broad drive to the house. The grey water lost its chill look, though something about the big grey house with its square, battlemented tower looking coldly to the north remained determinedly aloof.

They drove to a side entrance, and the chauffeur took her case again and opened the door for her.

"I hope you'll like it here," he said in a pleasant, amiable voice.

Rhona smiled at him wanly without replying, and he led the way across the tiled floor of a small hall to a door facing them. Her heart began to hammer painfully in her side, and the palms of her hands became suddenly moist. This, then, was the moment of her ordeal! She drew herself up with a little unconscious movement of defiance. She would meet Alan's mother as she meant to meet everyone else in this house—with a brave front.

But it was not Mrs. Hector Mailland who rose from the comfortable arm-chair beside the open stone hearth of the little parlour into which she was ushered, and laid her sewing aside to come forward with a friendly smile. It was a middle-aged woman of medium height in a severely cut grey dress with a neat stitched linen collar showing snowy-white at the high neckline. She had straight, iron-grey hair drawn back tightly into a neat pad at the back of her head which gave it a broader look than nature had intended until it appeared a solid frame for the kindly face. Her eyes were set wide apart above high cheekbones and they were vividly blue.

"This is Mrs. Norris, our housekeeper," the chauffeur intimated, withdrawing to leave Rhona standing in the middle of the little parlour looking surprised and relieved and uncertain all at once.

"Come over to the fire," invited Mrs. Norris, pushing forward a chair. "I'm glad to meet you, Miss Grant, and I hope you'll be happy here. Nurse Brodie will be in at half-past four," she went on, "and she will show you over the nurseries. Meantime, you will have tea with me this afternoon."

Rhona, a little taken aback by this unexpected encounter, yet strangely relieved by the homely presence of the housekeeper, sat down on the chair facing Mrs. Norris while a maid entered with the tea-tray.

"You'll be tired after your journey, I expect," Mrs. Norris remarked kindly enough, "so just sit back and have a rest while you can, wee dear. You'll be busy enough in all conscience once Nurse gets back." Her full lips tightened perceptibly. "You know your duties, of course," she added tersely, "and you'll be expected to do every one of them thoroughly under Nurse Brodie."

"Yes," Rhona said eagerly. "I suppose I've

arrived just when—just when the baby is out for his afternoon walk?"

Mrs. Norris nodded.

"You'll have to be resigned to loneliness at Kindarroch," she went on after a pause. "There's not a great deal to do for a young woman like yourself, but"—she hesitated, considering Rhona thoughtfully for a moment—"I don't think you're the type that will be easily discouraged."

Rhona found herself glancing at the clock on the mantelpiece.

"Isn't there something I could be doing before they come back—something in the nursery, I mean?"

Mrs. Norris looked surprised at the question, and then smiled.

"I like to see eagerness," she remarked, "and if it isn't just a temporary gusto I think you'll suit Mrs. Mailland all right. She demands service of the first order."

"I will do my best to give it," Rhona said firmly.

"I'll take you up to your room if you like," Mrs. Norris offered. "Fraser will have carried up your baggage by now."

She rose and crossed to the door, and Rhona was on her feet in an instant, following her out. Her impatience to see the nursery almost goaded her to run on ahead of the stout figure of the housekeeper as they re-crossed the hall and went up by a narrow oak stairway to the first floor. From the broad landing above doors led on either side, but her guide passed them all, going on to the end of the corridor where a stout wooden door barred their further progress.

"Here we are," Mrs. Norris intimated, opening it to reveal a short passage where the white enamel of the paintwork stood out in startling contrast to the old oak beams and heavy doors which seemed to be a feature of Kindarroch even in the back corridor by which Rhona had entered her husband's home.

She could not help smiling at the irony of the situation, and stepped over the threshold into a new world.

It was a world where someone had evidently taken pains to do everything correctly from the series of bright yellow ducks that waddled life-like across the green and white frieze of the day nursery down to the last fitting of the miniature bathroom with its spotless tiles and chromium plating. Rhona's heart warmed at the scene, stirring to new life within her. Surely people who had welcomed her son to this extent could not be really unkind? She stood in the cool, blue and white sanctuary of the night-nursery and drew in a deep breath of appreciation.

"It is all so lovely," she whispered, her eyes suddenly dim with unshed tears.

Mrs. Norris turned further along the corridor.

"Mrs. Mailland wouldn't have it otherwise. You will find that everything at Kindarroch is—just right, Miss Grant."

A narrow passage led off to the right, and at the end of it Mrs. Norris flung open a door.

"This is your room. It's not very big, but it's considered comfortable enough, and you'll find plenty of space for your clothes in the curtained alcove over there. It's part of the tower, but don't be afraid that it might be damp. The walls are three feet thick here."

Rhona passed into the tiny room where her suit-case had been deposited on a chair at the foot of the narrow iron bedstead. The floor was stained and polished a dark oak colour, and a plain deal dressing-chest was the only article of furniture apart from a wicker chair and a small writing-table beneath the high arched window.

Mrs. Norris turned back along the passage and, as Rhona joined her, a woman's voice came from the direction of the stairway at the far end of the suite of rooms. With flushed cheeks and a rapidly quickening pulse she realised that the newcomer was talking to a child. Robin!

The word almost escaped her parted lips, and then she stood still and just gazed along the corridor to where her son advanced in the arms of his nurse. The whole universe seemed to have stopped functioning, and only Robin's little wind-kissed face was visible to her hungry eyes. She drank in every detail of him, noting the minutest change. He was noticing more readily; he was taller, she thought. Could he stand yet, and not topple over as he did on the carpet at Giffnock?

Voices seemed to be coming to her from a great distance, and she heard Molly Grant's name—no, her own name now! With a supreme effort she dragged her eyes from her son's face and met those of the woman who held him in her arms.

Nurse Brodie was a tall woman in her middle thirties with a splendid carriage and good features marred only by too full lips which at this moment were endeavouring to compress themselves into a line of annoyance. She was regarding her new assistant with evident disfavour, and desperately Rhona realised that she had made a bad first impression. Her senior spoke sharply.

"If you'll remove your hat and get an apron, Grant, you can commence your duties at once."

She turned away with the child in her arms, and went quickly into the day-nursery.

Rhona fled along the narrow passage to her room, not because she had been stung by the curt order but because her eager hands were aching to do something for that white-clad bundle who had smiled Robin's slow smile, bringing all his dimples into play for her alone.

Of course, he did not remember, she told herself, and yet her heart beat high with a wondering doubt.

Might there not be something familiar about her even to one so young?

She was back in the nursery with her apron before Mrs. Norris had taken her departure, and the housekeeper smiled at her encouragingly as she closed the door behind her.

"And now," said Nurse Brodie in her most business-like tone, "you can undress Robin while I take off my hat and coat."

Rhona's heart was too full for speech as she stretched out her arms for her son, steeling herself to take him without clasping him closely to her breast, though the temptation to do so was wellnigh unbearable. She could not even trust herself to speak to him, though he looked up at her trustfully. She gazed hungrily down into the blue eyes as if she would never be able to assuage the longing within her by merely looking.

"Take off his outdoor things," Nurse Brodie prompted. "My dear girl, you'll learn that you can't sit gazing at a child for long. There's far too much work to do for that." She frowned. "You look stiff—awkward. Have you handled young children before?"

Rhona swallowed, and replied with an effort, trying to force her voice to a casual note:

"I've handled them much younger than this, Nurse."

"I wish you looked more like it, then," Enid Brodie declared bluntly though not unkindly. "If it's nervousness, the sooner you get over that the better, since you're here on a month's probation."

Rhona bit her lip feeling that she was looking more nervous than ever, and began to fumble with the buttons of a familiar coat. And then, because it *was* a familiar coat—the white woollen jacket in which her son had journeyed from the bungalow—time and place dropped from her, and she forgot even the critical eyes of her superior as she performed

39

a task she had done a thousand times—was it yesterday or a hundred years ago?

When he had been freed from his white leggings the child made a movement towards the floor, and she realised that he could stand. Holding on to one hand, she led him gravely round the corner of the blue playpen towards the table by the window where he relinquished his hold on her finger with a little gurgling laugh and stood up independently beside his own chair.

"Clever boy!" she encouraged. "Oh, what a clever Robin!"

She knelt down beside him, sitting back on her heels, her face radiant as she watched him make his uncertain way round the high chair, and for a moment or two neither moved nor spoke but just sat looking her fill.

"Are you a day-dreamer, Grant?" The curt voice cut in upon her happy thoughts and she rose hastily to her feet to confront her superior. "If so," Nurse Brodie added acidly, "there's no room for you here. When I have changed Robin there will probably be some washing to see to. You'll find a hand-basin for that purpose in the bathroom, and it's your duty to tidy up here as soon as tea is over. Mrs. Mailland comes to the nursery to say good-night at six o'clock sharp and everything must be in apple-pie order before then."

Rhona lifted the woolly coat and leggings.

"If you'll tell me where these go," she began.

"Top drawer of the chest there." Nurse Brodie nodded across the room. "You'll find his pyjamas and dressing-gown in the bottom one."

Rhona turned to her task of preparing the bath, but now her thoughts were clouded by the approaching ordeal of the meeting with her mother-in-law. From many little inferences she had already gathered that Mrs. Mailland was a stickler for detail and that she would not permit tardy service. The six o'clock visit to the nursery seemed more like a tour of inspection than any demonstration of affection for her grandson, and as the hour drew nearer, Rhona's heart almost failed her.

Catherine Mailland announced her arrival by a sharp knock and came quickly into the nursery as if almost expecting to meet some delinquency. Rhona got up from her knees where she had been folding socks into their special drawer in the blue enamel chest, and looked across the room.

Her mother-in-law's features were already familiar to her through the photographs which Alan had possessed, but no portrait could do full justice to this handsome woman since it left out the beauty of her colouring which had not faded with the years. Titian red hair and a flawless skin with hardly a wrinkle made Mrs. Hector Mailland look many years younger than her actual age, and her features and carriage were truly regal. The whole effect would have been a worthy picture of aristocratic charm but for the coldly remote look in the grey-green eyes which measured the new servant in her household with evident doubt.

"Yes, of course," she remarked distantly, as if she were inspecting a necessary but uninteresting piece of furniture, "You're the new nurse." She turned to the older woman who was holding her grandson, though she made no attempt to speak to the child. "I hope you will find her suitable, Nurse," she said. "Remember, any complaints must come straight to me. I won't have bickerings." She gave Rhona another searching look, and then dismissed her altogether as she glanced round the nursery, her keen eyes missing nothing. "You won't forget about to-morrow, Nurse," she remarked on her way back to the door. "I think I told you that I want Sir Ranald and Lady

41

Margaret to see my grandson on his very best behaviour."

Rhona felt a hot surge of anger rising within her and, as the white door closed on the regal figure of her mother-in-law, she glanced across at Nurse Brodie, and saw some of her sentiments reflected in the older woman's small, resentful eyes.

"Old Tartar!" Enid Brodie exploded viciously, her dignity suddenly shed. "All she cares about is the precious Mailland name! She hasn't an ounce of genuine affection for this little chap in the whole of her body!"

Rhona felt the colour receding from her cheeks. "No—surely!" she protested.

Nurse Brodie collected her discarded dignity.

"Possibly I should not have put it like that," she said rather frigidly to cover her still smouldering rage, "but Mrs. Mailland invariably rubs me the wrong way. She has no need to come up here and tell me my duty. As if I would take the child down to the drawing-room looking a fright!"

She rose with Robin in her arms, smiling quite fondly and with a proprietary air that touched Rhona's sensitive heart and made it warm to this woman whose quick-tempered speech had found an echo within her, though she knew that Nurse Brodie had regretted the indignity immediately, and would not let her outburst serve as a loophole for future familiarity on the part of her junior.

"You'd better forget about Mrs. Mailland and get on with your duties," she observed sharply. "Though *I* am finished up here as soon as Robin is put to bed, you have quite a lot to do, and the sooner you clear up the nursery and prepare for the morning the sooner you will be free."

Rhona watched her son being carried from the room in the other's arms, her heart lighter within her than it had been for many weeks, and she turned

42

to her menial tasks as happily as if life had started for her anew.

When she had put Robin to bed, and closed the door of the night-nursery behind her, Nurse Brodie paused before going into her own sitting-room.

"Oh, by the way, Grant," she remarked, "when you're finished in the nursery the remainder of the evening is your own, but I'd advise you if you do go out for a walk to be in early. You rise at quarter to six in the morning, and make my tea before the baby wakens—generally somewhere round about six o'clock. You'd better set the alarm in your room." She was about to turn away when her eyes rested on the oak door at the far end of the corridor. "I may as well tell you about that doorway while I remember," she added. "On no account must it be left open. The staircase leads through the tower and it is broken in places. The baby might quite easily injure himself if he were to stray there now that he is attempting to walk. I want you to remember that Grant. It is most important."

"Yes, Nurse."

As if she would forget! Rhona thought, and wondered why such a danger was left unrepaired.

Her tasks took her another hour, and at half-past seven she surveyed the day-nursery and the spotless bathroom beyond and decided that even Mrs. Mailland would be hard pressed to find anything out of place in Robin's shining domain.

It had been a long day, but, curiously enough, she was not tired. The sight of her son had refreshed her spirit, and it had been in spirit that she had been so cast down. Now the desire within her to do her work faithfully and so remain near him was coupled with the desire to see more of her new surroundings, and she decided that, even before she unpacked her suitcase, she would go out for an hour and make herself familiar with the immediate neighbourhood.

She turned in the direction of her own room and her way took her past the night-nursery where Robin lay asleep. She lingered at the door, hesitated, and stood still. Dare she look in at him?

Cautiously she turned the handle and opened the door. A muslin curtain wavered at the window and the clear, sweet smell of pines pervaded the big, airy room as she stood there looking in at her child. How beautiful he looked, lying there on his back with both arms flung upwards in that familiar attitude, his chubby fists loosely closed, his lips parted a little as if he smiled in his sleep. It was thus he had lain contentedly in the bungalow at Giffnock——

A strange sensation of being watched broke coldly across the roseate glow of her dream, and she turned from the nursery door to find herself confronted by a tall, angular young woman in tweeds who observed her frowningly from the end of the corridor outside the oak doorway leading to the tower. Rhona fancied that the newcomer must have entered by the forbidden stairway as no one had passed along the corridor while she had stood outside Robin's room.

She was quite sure that this tall, rather disdainful creature with the cold, grey eyes was one of the family—Gertrude Mailland, she guessed instinctively.

"Has the child been awake?" the newcomer asked sharply. "Surely you know better than to go to him even if he cried a little?"

Rhona, looking up into the grey eyes, could scarcely suppress an involuntary shiver. There was something about this woman that she disliked.

Gertrude Mailland was not a beautiful woman like her mother—her height and angular body made her seem awkward—but she was a striking-looking woman for all that. Her features were regular enough, though her skin was sallow and, allied to raven black hair parted severely in the centre, gave her almost a slavonic look. Only her eyes, pale grey and curiously repelling, confused the suggestion.

Rhona found herself looking into those pale eyes with a feeling which was akin to apprehension.

"No," she said slowly, "Robin wasn't awake. I looked in to see—just to see him."

Something like a sneer twisted the older woman's lips and her thin mouth took on an even harder line.

"So you're one of the baby-worshipping kind!" She laughed unpleasantly. "Well, don't let Nurse Brodie catch you, or you'll be using your return ticket to Glasgow long before the end of the month." She had been watching Rhona closely as she spoke and did not miss the dull flush that rose in her cheeks at the threat of dismissal. "Isn't it your time off?" she enquired a fraction less coldly. "Brodie mustn't keep you doing her work all evening while she reads her damned trashy novels, you know."

The remark spoke only too plainly of Gertrude Mailland's active dislike of Enid Brodie and a queer, chill feeling clutched at Rhona's heart as she thought of her son surrounded by such open enmity.

"Nurse Brodie told me I might go out into the grounds for an hour before supper." Her clear, deep voice echoed across a gulf which seemed to have opened out between Gertrude Mailland and herself. "I was just going down."

The older woman's pale eyes narrowed, the look in them becoming almost crafty. Her smile was slow, calculating and plainly ingratiating as she turned towards the door leading to the tower.

"You'll find it much quicker to go down this way, Grant," she said. "The stairs are safe enough if you are careful, and it is still quite light."

Rhona's lips were curiously dry as she objected with quick vehemence.

"I have just been warned not to use that stairway. If the door was left open Robin might fall——"

In her anxiety and fear for her son she had cast discretion to the winds, and Gertrude Mailland watched her with a curiously intent expression in her pale eyes.

"You seem strangely attached to the child already," she observed. "More of that sickening sentiment where the heir to Kindarroch is concerned, I suppose!"

The scorn in her tone had deepened to actual antipathy and Rhona stood gazing at her aghast, seeing down into this woman's meagre soul and remembering a sentence out of the past as if it had been spoken again in that quiet corridor.

'If anything happens to me and I pass out without an heir, Kindarroch goes to Gertrude.'

Alan—her husband—had said that, and now it came rushing back to her with a force that made her feel as if the very ground was rocking beneath her feet. Gertrude Mailland, but for Robin, would have owned Kindarroch one day, and because of her thwarted hopes and her lust for possession, she hated the child who stood in her way.

The thought was too staggering to be admitted at once, and it was only a vague sense of it which Rhona grasped as she stood looking into the pale eyes of her sister-in-law. Perturbed and shaken by the impression she could not wholly erase from her mind, she turned towards the inner stairway, and knew a feeling of relief as Gertrude Mailland moved away from the nursery door.

CHAPTER THREE

A WEEK slipped past on winged feet and yet, reviewing that week, Rhona realised that it had been crowded with impressions and that now almost the entire household at Kindarroch was dovetailed in her mind with all their peculiarities: the little, secretive kindnesses of Hector Mailland, who had been the greatest surprise to her of them all, and who was still a vague, almost unreal shadow flitting in the background of life at Kindarroch, out there in the woods most of his time listening to the feathered songsters he knew by name, eager to welcome a newcomer among the trees, living a life apart with those dumb friends who knew and understood him better than any human creature; the arrogance of Gertrude where her own wishes were concerned, and her bursts of ungovernable temper; Nurse Brodie's preoccupation with her light novel-reading which she frequently permitted to interfere with her duties; the housekeeper's brief smiles of encouragement whenever they met, and, finally, the sharp criticisms of Mrs. Mailland herself.

It was a strange household, but Rhona was content within the grey walls because, for a few hours each day, she came actively into contact with her son. Though her tasks were the most menial, she guarded them jealously, and if she were left alone with Robin for a moment it contented her for the rest of the day.

Her first task in the morning after she had tidied up the nurseries was to clean and polish the handsome new perambulator which Mrs. Mailland had considered only fitting for the heir to Kindarroch. It dwarfed its poor little counterpart hidden away behind the trunks in the cupboard at Giffnock, but Rhona's heart held no resentment. She polished and dusted with a will until even Nurse Brodie remarked that it was a pleasure to wheel the child out in it.

And the pleasure was always hers, for Rhona's tasks finished at the polishing.

This afternoon, however, it seemed that they were longer in coming down to the terrace, and

Rhona rearranged the cushion twice before the parlourmaid came out with the message that Nurse Brodie wanted her upstairs immediately.

She found her senior seated on a chair in the day-nursery with one of her endless novels open on her knees while Robin sat fully dressed in his high chair. Nurse Brodie had not attempted to put on her out-door clothes and her feet were still thrust into the soft slippers she wore in the house.

"You may wheel the baby out this afternoon, Grant," she announced. "I don't feel equal to it."

Rhona's heart leapt with sheer joy, and then a cloud dimmed the shining eyes.

"But—Mrs. Mailland, Nurse? I thought——"

"You're not paid to think!" Enid Brodie snapped, and then, relenting a little: "They're out this after-noon—both of them. They won't be back until after six."

Rhona knew that she was referring to her mother-in-law and Gertrude. Hector Mailland was never taken into anyone's calculations, though most of the domestic staff would have run a mile to serve him had he ever expressed a wish to be served.

"Make yourself presentable in case you meet any of the neighbours," Nurse Brodie cautioned as she picked up her novel and stretched out her feet. "And don't be later than four-thirty. Have you got a watch?"

"Yes," Rhona answered on her way along the corridor to her own room.

She changed into her navy-blue coat and the plain felt hat which Molly had chosen for her, but its unflattering severity could not dull the look in her eyes nor banish the smile of tenderness from her sensitive mouth as she fled back to the nursery to carry her son downstairs for the first time.

"Oh, Robin!" she whispered, her lips close against the soft cheek, "won't it be heavenly—just you and I together, at last! We'll look for birds and little fish in the loch, and you'll see the sheep and the cows coming down to the water to drink——!"

She laughed aloud in her happiness, holding him to her a moment longer before she finally sat him in his pram.

"There!" she said. "Which way shall we go?"

Robin looked at her expectantly, smiling his appreciation.

"Away round the top of the loch?" she asked. "It's lovely there, and you can't see Kindarroch at all when you're in among the trees. . . ."

The road she had chosen was narrow and white-sanded in places where it came near to the water's edge, and the wheels of the pram turned noiselessly on its soft surface.

Walking quickly for over half an hour, she came to the head of the loch, and there her pace slackened and she went along by the edge of the water, eager to grasp every moment's happiness out of this unexpected pleasure.

The face of things had miraculously changed, and the vague feeling of some sinister undercurrent at Kindarroch melted before the sunshine of simple pleasure. The beauty of her surroundings was manifest to her as never before. The silence of the glen was the silence of birdsong, of a wind soughing gently among the pines, of a brown burn flowing over little white stones—

She talked to her child as she had never been able to do at Kindarroch, eagerly, openly, and Robin responded with smiles and gurgles of delight, his chubby hands clapping his applause.

They continued thus for over a mile until, rounding a bend, they came upon a man in nut-brown tweeds crouched close beside the thick beech hedge which girdled the pinewood.

Rhona started, but soon she was smiling as the bent figure straightened, and looked round at her with a friendly expression in his deep blue eyes. He held a feathery bundle between his hands, and he walked over to the pram with it.

"Hullo, young man!" he greeted Robin. "What do you think Grandpa has here? Would you like to look?"

Robin stretched out an eager hand, but Hector Mailland shook his head.

"He's been hurt, sonny. I'm afraid you can't hold him just yet. One day we must teach you to hold little birds gently, and then, when you call to them, they will come to you just as they do to Grandpa."

He straightened from the pram to look at Rhona.

"I found him entangled in the undergrowth," he explained, stroking the feathery head.

Rhona touched the tiny head with a gently caressing finger, and the beady eyes darted at her suspiciously, though the bird made no effort to escape from between Hector Mailland's cupped hands.

"Poor little thing," she said softly. "Is it badly hurt?"

"Oh, no! Just exhausted. In a little while he will fly away."

"You love birds," she said, all the shyness which she had felt in that first moment of their meeting evaporating before his kindly smile. "And how easily they come to you! They must know."

"I think they do," he said, "after a bit. Though some of them are very timid. I have lain for hours in the undergrowth here trying to get a bluetit near enough to photograph."

The captive linnet moved, trying to stretch its cramped wings, and instantly Hector Mailland opened his hands. The little creature did not rise

50

into the air immediately, but, with the utmost confidence, sat on his brown palm until it felt ready to take off.

Hector Mailland turned back to the pram.

"He'll probably come next time I call—just to say 'thank you'!"

"Will you know him?" Rhona asked.

"I think so." He smiled down into her dark eyes. "How are you liking it here?" he asked abruptly and rather doubtfully.

"I love it," Rhona told him truthfully, feeling instinctively that she could be perfectly natural with this man who seemingly counted for so little under his own roof, but who, she thought, was the most human and kindly old gentleman she had ever met. "I don't think I have ever seen lovelier countryside," she added.

"It can compare with the best," he said with justifiable pride. "Our side of the loch is often considered rather stern, but I think austerity has its beauty, don't you?"

He appealed to her as an equal, not talking down to her as a servant as Gertrude and her mother had done, and Rhona was human enough to appreciate the fact. Her heart warmed to him, and all her harsh thoughts of him in the past were dispelled in a great wave of kindred feeling.

"Yes, I like grandeur as long as there are trees to go with it. It's bare rock that overawes one a bit, like—like the Cuillins on Skye."

"Ah, you've been to Skye!" He walked forward beside the pram and began to discuss the Misty Isle with a fervour that awakened a reciprocal feeling in Rhona's breast, for her mother had been born on the island, and its ties had stretched out to encircle the daughter of her Lowland marriage.

He told her that he had seen his first golden eagle there, and she said, with a smile, that she didn't suppose it had come down and eaten out of his hand, and they laughed at that, making Robin laugh too, and clap his fat hands in glee.

"I like the name my son and his wife chose for the boy," Mailland said suddenly, and Rhona felt the colour receding from her cheeks, leaving her pale and shaken at this first direct reference to herself by a Mailland.

"Yes," she managed. "Yes—it is very pretty. It is a nice name for a little boy, but I often wonder if it won't be rather—awkward when he grows older——"

She broke off sharply, realising that she had made a mistake, that she had spoken to Hector Mailland as Robin's mother. Looking quickly at the bronzed, lined face of the man walking slowly by her side, she realised that he hadn't noticed anything amiss.

"I don't think so," he said. "It is a good name, plain and quite manly."

Her cheeks glowed. How kind he was!

They had walked a considerable distance round the head of the loch and now, as they rounded a bend in the winding road, the west side came into full view. The sun shone down on a silvery stretch of sand curving in a miniature bay and, beyond, a green slope of rich pasture led to a white, one-storeyed house with tall chimneys that caught the sun and seemed to send it back reflected doubly in the green water. Grey rocks shut in this tiny beach on either side, accentuating the tranquillity of the retreat, and dark pines hovered in the background, screening it from the wind from the west.

"Oh!" Rhona caught her breath. "How lovely it is!"

"Yes," he said, "it is an ideally situated house. Dulmore Lodge, it is called."

Robin claimed his attention again, and Rhona turned the pram in the direction of Kindarroch, though even as she turned her back on the peaceful bay on the other side of the loch she seemed to feel the call of the simple white house pulling at her heart.

Hector Mailland walked with her to the boundary of the estate, and there a car drew up and the man in it hailed him from the far side of the road. Rhona walked on, realising that she had gone farther in his company than time had permitted, and that it was now well after half-past four.

Enid Brodie was waiting for her on the top step of the side door, and she was frowning.

"I thought I told you to be back promptly?" she began.

"I'm sorry," Rhona apologised as she undid the safety-strap round Robin's waist. "I'm afraid I walked a little too far round the loch. It was such a lovely day."

"Don't stand there talking," her senior repri-manded. "Get the child in quickly. They've come back—sooner than I expected."

She hustled Rhona inside, but before they had gained the staircase, the green baize dividing door at the far end of the hall swung open, and Gertrude Mailland stood confronting them.

She measured them both with her cold grey eyes, one glance taking in the situation, and then she smiled sardonically, delighting, it seemed, in their discomfort, Rhona experienced an almost over-whelming urge to run up the stairs with Robin in her arms, but Enid Brodie's hand on her arm detained her, and she stood her ground.

"What is the meaning of this?" Gertrude rapped out, her pale eyes on the older woman's set face. "Perhaps you can explain it, Nurse?"

Enid Brodie took a deep breath.

"I shall explain," she said stiffly, "when I am asked for an explanation by Mrs. Mailland."

Gertrude's sallow cheeks flushed a dull red and the colour rose in an unbecoming wave to her forehead.

Her temper was evidently almost out of control.

"You have adopted this attitude more than once, Nurse," she reminded angrily, "and I have refrained from mentioning your insubordination to my mother, but I'll see that she hears of this afternoon's episode. I suppose"—sarcastically—"you thought we were safely out of the way for an hour or two, and you took the opportunity of lazing around with one of your everlasting novels. Or perhaps," she suggested vindictively, "you took the chance of going into Darroch to see Doctor Inglis?"

Rhona, seeing Robin's sensitive lip beginning to tremble at the sound of the angry voices, began to walk slowly up the stairs, but not before she had heard Enid Brodie's reply to that last remark.

"There's nothing to stop you from thinking what you like, Miss Mailland, but not even your mother has a right to interfere in my friendship with Doctor Inglis or anyone else."

Rhona fled up the remaining stairs and, out of earshot at last, drew in a deep breath. What would happen now? Instant dismissal for herself and a severe reprimand for Nurse Brodie, who had not sought to implicate her in any way? Her heart was beating fastly when her senior followed her into the room, anger in every line of her stiffened form.

"I'm awfully sorry, Nurse," Rhona began. "It was all my fault. If only I had not been those few minutes late, but—I met Robin's grandfather at the head of the loch and we walked further than I realised."

Enid Brodie glanced at her curiously.

"Oh, you met old Mailland? Well, anyway, that wouldn't have mattered. *He* wouldn't have given us away." She tossed her head defiantly. "Not that I care two straws!" she declared unconcernedly. "Mrs. Mailland can please herself about what she does, and if she's in the mood we'll both get our notice."

"Surely not for such a little thing?" Rhona protested. "Besides, they couldn't very well leave Robin without a nurse."

"No. Nurses are not so easy to get nowadays," Enid Brodie admitted. "That's why you were engaged on your references alone without an exhaustive interview. You were needed here, and you were the only applicant."

Rhona flushed.

"I see," she said, but Enid Brodie was too busy with her own thoughts to notice the awkwardness of the pause which followed.

"As for Miss Gertrude," she went on furiously, "I'll thank her to mind her own business. I was engaged by Mrs. Mailland, and I take my orders direct from the mistress of the house." She flounced across the floor and began to spread the cloth on the nursery table—a job which was really Rhona's. "As for interfering in my private affairs," she went on, "I won't have it. It's not the first time she's tried to pry into my friendship with Jim Inglis, and it's just like her to suggest that it's an illicit love affair and that I'm making the running."

Rhona was beginning to feel decidedly uncomfortable, and she rose and carried Robin across to his chair, thinking that tea would stem the torrent of her senior's wrath. But the avalanche had been launched on its downward course, carrying discretion and dignity with it.

"As if she had any room to talk!" Nurse Brodie continued scathingly: "If she's not mistress of Dulmore Lodge before long it won't be her fault!"

"Dulmore Lodge?" Rhona repeated, interested. "That's the house on the other side of the loch, isn't it?"

"Yes. It belongs to an Edinburgh family of solicitors. They only come here part of the year, but

Neil Murray is living there now because he has had an accident."

Neil Murray! Rhona started at the mention of the familiar name. Neil Murray at Dulmore Lodge, just across the loch!

She laughed rather forlornly. What use to worry now about the result of this afternoon's adventure, when her dismissal would be instantaneous the moment Neil Murray saw her and her deception was revealed to the Maillands!

She felt that she hated Neil Murray for all he stood for. It was he who had come to her in the name of the Maillands, advising her to let Robin go, she reflected bitterly, adding that he had acted solely to further a business obligation. The Maillands were his clients and so, she reasoned, he had sought to bend her to their will. And now he could break her utterly by the knowledge he held.

Desperately she told herself that she must avoid him as long as possible, and found consolation in the thought that it might not be too difficult to do so since she scarcely went out of the grounds in the evenings when she was free.

She completed her tasks automatically, glancing occasionally at the silent form of Enid Brodie whose brows were still creased in the dark frown which Gertrude's tirade had produced. She was obviously brooding over the whole affair, and it was plain to be seen that she resented Gertrude's interference and had no intention of giving way before it.

When the parlourmaid appeared in place of Mrs. Mailland at six o'clock, she forestalled the girl by remarking acidly:

"I suppose Mrs. Mailland wants to see me?"

The girl nodded.

"Tell her I'll be down immediately." Nurse Brodie's lips were a thin, pale line.

It was a flourish, and Rhona was quick to realise it—quick, also, to see the look of strain behind the arrogance in the other's eyes.

"Please," she said, when Robin was safely in his cot and the nursery door closed for the night, "let me take part of the blame, Nurse. I should have been back when you said."

"It's not a question of blame," Enid Brodie returned, drawing herself up to her full height. "You did as you were told. It's a question of whom *I'm* to take orders from. I'll admit I need this job, but I'm not going to be brow-beaten by Gertrude Mailland."

She swept out of the room, and Rhona returned to her task of tidying the day-nursery with a heavy heart. In a minute or two she also would be called to account in the study, and her mother-in-law would be able to find the first fault in her service. That Mrs. Mailland would consider it a major one was only to be expected.

The minutes dragged past, however, and at seven o'clock heavy footsteps on the stairs proclaimed Enid Brodie's return. Rhona stood waiting, but she passed the nursery and went on to her own sitting-room, slamming the door behind her with a viciousness that evidently reflected her turbulent thoughts.

The following day no reference was made to the incident. Enid Brodie was evidently in one of her most difficult moods, disinclined to talk, and going about her tasks with a grim efficiency which imparted a chill air to the nursery atmosphere and froze Rhona's questions on her lips.

"It's my afternoon off, Grant," she intimated just before lunch, "and I mean to take it. They can think what they like. I'm entitled to it."

"And I—take Robin out?"

"Oh, yes. It's quite official this afternoon!"

Nurse Brodie put on her outdoor uniform and left shortly after two o'clock for what appeared to be an appointment, and Rhona knew that she would not be back until late. She had forgotten for the moment about her mother-in-law's inspection of the nurseries, and she set off for her walk with a happy heart.

"We'll go the same way again," she said to the child, "and look for Grandpa's little bird!" and it was not until she was well over a mile from Kindarroch that she remembered that she had chosen the way which led to Dulmore Lodge.

The thought, when it presented itself, made her halt in the middle of the road, uncertain whether to turn back or go on, now that she had come so far. Then, as if a third course was being laid open to her, she saw a narrow pathway leading down through a glade of silver birch to the shores of the loch.

She took it almost as if she were being pursued, pushing the pram down the incline under the trees, and eventually onto a narrow strip of pebbly beach.

It was quiet here, with an open view of the loch, and the screen of trees between her and the road where at any moment, it seemed, she might come face to face with the one man in all this broad countryside who knew her identity. Such a fear would be ever present now, she thought unhappily. It would haunt her at every turn until at last she met Neil Murray.

Well, why dwell on such a possibility to-day? Let to-morrow look after itself, she decided with a happy smile as she lifted Robin out of his pram and set him down on his uncertain little legs.

They played together for the best part of an hour, mother and son again, with no one to deny her her right and only the little grey leaves of the birches above them whispering to the light wind blowing in from the loch. Now and then a pale gold leaf fluttered to the ground and she caught it between her hands for the child, so that he gurgled his delight and stumbled and fell into her arms, where she held him undetected against her breast.

"Oh, Robin darling! Robin!" she breathed. "Why couldn't it be like this always? Just you and I here beside the blue water and the little leaves falling down on us like gentle rain——!"

Her voice choked and she buried her head in the white woolly coat.

When she looked up at last the face of the loch had undergone a change: the blue had given place to grey, and a small boat was coming diagonally across to the bay where they had taken refuge. It was propelled by a man, a single oarsman whose broad figure, even at that distance, was strangely familiar.

In a flash she realised that the boat had come from the direction of Dulmore Lodge, and that the oarsman was Neil Murray.

Panic-stricken, she rose to her feet and put Robin back into his pram, her one desire being to escape before the boat came near enough for the man in it to see and recognise her.

The return journey was not so easy as the descent had been, however, and with a little quiver of dismay she felt the wheels settling down into the mud. She pushed, but the incline onto the road was steeper than she thought, and Robin was a heavy child. The pram moved a few inches and then slipped back, and she stood gazing at it helplessly, her ears straining for the grating of a keel on the pebbly shore behind them.

Turning the pram, she made a last effort to pull it up the bank, and so intent was she upon her task that she failed to hear the sound of an approaching car, and was hardly even aware of it when it pulled up beside her on the road.

"You look as if you might need some manly assistance down there!" a voice observed, and she looked up to find the occupant of the car getting out of the driver's seat.

"Oh, thank you!" Her voice was full of her obvious relief. "I had no idea it would be so difficult to get back or I would never have gone down."

The stranger pulled the pram onto the roadway with the minimum of effort, and she looked at his big, square frame and wondered who he was. Then she remembered having seen the car before, only yesterday, when it had drawn up at the Kindarroch boundary and Hector Mailland had excused himself to go over and speak to the driver.

"And how is Robin?" the big man was asking, as if he intended to linger. "Still liking his new home?"

A flush which she was quite powerless to control spread over Rhona's cheeks, and her eyes wavered and fell before the direct look in his twinkling blue ones. He evidently misjudged her confusion, for he said with an impersonal note in his voice:

"I'm Robin's doctor—though, so far, he hasn't needed my services."

"Oh, you're Doctor Inglis?"

He smiled more broadly.

"The same!"

Rhona stood hesitating, the thought of the man out there on the loch behind them goading her to make her escape.

"I'm rather late," she began lamely. "I must get back to Kindarroch before half-past four."

Doctor Inglis glanced at his wrist-watch.

"You'll easily manage it," he told her.

He continued to look at her with a friendly scrutiny which Rhona felt suddenly embarrassing, though she knew that here was a man who, in the ordinary way, she would have liked immediately.

"I must go, all the same," she said. "I don't want to be late."

"It's Nurse Brodie's afternoon off, isn't it?" he observed unexpectedly. "A minute or two wouldn't really matter."

"Mrs. Mailland dislikes bad time-keeping," Rhona said, settling Robin's cover.

"I know," he returned gravely, "and I won't keep you if you really think you should be on your way." He turned to Robin, though Rhona had the impression that he was still observing her though he was no longer looking directly at her. "Well, good-bye, young man! And see that you behave yourself now that you have such a capable nurse!"

Rhona, her mind on the man behind them who might even now be beaching his boat in the little bay she had just left, smiled faintly at the compliment and hurried on, the feeling of overwhelming relief at her escape making her run the last few yards to the gates.

There, however, she drew up sharply, for Gertrude Mailland was standing in the middle of the carriage-way, where she had dismounted from her bicycle, and her narrowed eyes were bent on the pram where the marks of drying mud were only too plain to be seen.

"I thought I'd wait for you here, Grant," Miss Mailland observed. "Perhaps you can explain what took you down to the loch-side with the pram."

"It was quite warm this afternoon, and I thought it would be good for Robin to stretch his legs a little. It was much safer on the loch-side than on the main road," Rhona explained.

"Perhaps so," Gertrude allowed. "But what do you suppose the pram is going to look like when you pull it through a marshy wood every afternoon?"

Rhona ignored the exaggeration, saying diffidently:

"The mud will clean off once it is dry. I will do it to-night in my free time."

Gertrude returned to the attack from another direction.

"The pram wasn't exactly the main issue, Grant," she declared. "We must impress upon you that we won't have our servants talking to men when they are on duty." She remounted her machine with the air of having produced a trump card. "I shall certainly report the incident to my mother."

She rode off in the direction of the house before Rhona could explain who had come to her assistance, and there was nothing left to do but to follow in her wake.

Mrs. Mailland came to the nursery at a quarter to six that evening, and Rhona had just prepared Robin's bath when her tall figure blocked the doorway.

"Leave the child in the play-pen a moment or two, Grant," she ordered, "and come through to the night-nursery. I want to speak to you."

Her keen eyes had wandered round the room, observing each detail in her customary way, and she swept out, leaving the impression behind that she was amazed that all was in order.

The night-nursery was cool and pleasant, but, as she closed the door behind her, Rhona felt that it was stifling. Was this to be dismissal, instantaneous and final?

Her mother-in-law surveyed her coldly for several seconds before she spoke.

"I don't know what sort of place you were in before you came here, Grant," she began, "but if they permitted the conduct my daughter has just reported to me, I'm afraid their reference was not of great worth."

Rhona's heart began to beat wildly as she wondered if she would be expected to defend her last 'position,' of which she knew nothing. She sought about in her mind but could not even recall the name of Molly Lang's last employer.

"Well?" Mrs. Mailland demanded. "What have you to say?"

"About this afternoon?" Rhona met her eyes squarely. "I'm sorry about the pram, madam, but I shall clean it immediately. It is just a little mud, and I had no idea that it was marshy down that pathway."

"I am not concerned about the pram," Mrs. Mailland returned. "I was referring to the fact of you meeting some man or other. Surely you understand that such conduct will not be tolerated while you are on duty?"

Rhona smiled because of the sudden relief she felt.

"Oh," she said, "but that was Doctor Inglis. He stopped his car and offered to help when he saw that I was in difficulty."

Catherine Mailland's expression underwent a swift change. The cold look passed from her eyes to give place to one of anger.

"But Gertrude led me to understand——" she began, and then, branching off at a tangent, she sought to cover the mistake she had made. "Evidently I misunderstood my daughter," she said, "or she did not recognise the doctor's car. Nevertheless, that does not excuse you being on the loch-side where you had no right to be. You are paid to wheel my grandson out, not to laze about reading or daydreaming on the shore. I hope you understand me?"

"Perfectly, madam. I will walk with Robin if you prefer it." Rhona met the stern gaze unflinchingly. "I had no idea he was not to be taken out of his pram."

Catherine Mailland seemed to be really seeing her for the first time. She looked at her searchingly, then the indifferent expression returned to her face and she remarked coldly:

"Very well, Grant. I accept your apology. But make sure in future that you remember my edict about male acquaintances. I will not have you philandering while you are out with Robin, no matter who the man may be. The doctor, of course, is different."

Rhona's sense of humour asserted itself at this juncture and she wondered if her mother-in-law was giving her a free hand to philander with the doctor, but the suppressed smile evidently passed unnoticed by Catherine Mailland as she turned to the door.

"I have no complaint with the way you attend to your duty otherwise," she observed unexpectedly. "So far, you have been quite satisfactory, though I must admit I was doubtful of your ability at first."

It was late before Enid Brodie returned, and she did not seek Rhona out, but on the following morning she intimated, after a moody silence, that she would be away for an hour that afternoon again.

"I have some business to attend to," she said noncommittally. "Mrs. Mailland has given me permission to go."

Rhona could scarcely suppress her joy and satisfaction, and not even her senior's parting words could damp her anticipation of the afternoon.

"You'll probably not feel so elated at having Robin to yourself when you hear there's going to be company!" she said, rather sarcastically. "You get back from your walk at three o'clock on such occasions and change him. Then, when his presence is requested in the drawing-room, you take him down, and stand aside while Mrs. Mailland shows him off to the assembled guests and takes all the credit for his wonderful appearance!"

"Oh!" Rhona gasped, a little taken aback, but

that was all. Even this ordeal could be faced for the compensation of another afternoon alone with her son.

She returned from their walk promptly at three o'clock, and it was almost four when the parlourmaid came to summon her downstairs. Only then did her courage waver, but she gathered Robin up in her arms, and the touch of his soft skin against her cheek gave her heart again. After all, she would be very little in the picture.

It was the first time she had been in the main part of the house, and she looked round her with a certain curiosity as she followed the parlourmaid across the expanse of hall with its lofty oak beams and carved archways and the long, mullioned windows through which the afternoon sun streamed in a yellow beam. Here and there her footsteps died in the soft luxury of Turkish rugs, and at last they drew up before a great oak door.

"There isn't much company to-day," the parlourmaid smiled, as if Rhona's nervousness was quite understandable. "Just one gentleman."

She opened the door before Rhona could reply, and stepped aside to let her enter with the child.

The hum of conversation died down, leaving a silence that could almost be felt. Rhona stepped across the threshold with Robin in her arms, and was aware of a family gathering—Gertrude and her mother on the chesterfield at the window, Hector Mailland standing with his legs apart before the fire, and the one visitor seated in a chair with his back towards the door.

"Ah, here you are, Grant!" Mrs. Mailland got up and crossed the room, addressing the man in the chair. "Neil, this is Alan's son."

The visitor rose to his feet with the aid of a stick, and Rhona's heart seemed to turn over in her breast as she looked up into the grey eyes of the solicitor who had persuaded her to part with her child.

Neil Murray's surprise was perhaps greater than her own, but it passed in his eyes in a second as if in answer to that first agonising appeal in hers. Her arms tightened about Robin in a protective attitude. Surely this man would understand? And then something seemed to shatter inside her. How well he had 'understood' before when he had offered her the advice which had brought her to this pass! What use to expect understanding or even sympathy from him?

"Put the baby down, Grant," Mrs. Mailland commanded. "Well, Neil, there he is!"

Murray's eyes moved from Rhona's pale face and he smiled down at Robin.

"The heir to Kindarroch and, by the look of him, a worthy successor!" he said, quite deliberately turning his back upon Rhona and bending down to the child's level. "We must be great friends, my lad! Your dad and I were the best of pals, and we'll be near neighbours from now on since you've come for your heritage!"

Rhona caught sight of Gertrude seated on the chesterfield. Her face was livid, and the look of naked hatred which Neil Murray's words had lighted in the pale eyes made her look like some avenging fury. It passed, however, almost as quickly as it had come, but it had awakened again that vague feeling of uneasiness in Rhona's mind, the feeling that all was not well at Kindarroch.

Mrs. Mailland was on her favourite subject, explaining to the young solicitor how tremendously important it was that the Mailland name should continue at Kindarroch.

"It might so easily have been otherwise," she went on, an unaccustomed fire in her cold eyes, "and that they had the sense to provide us with an heir is the most that can be said for my son's marriage. The child has Mailland blood in him."

Rhona stood immovable, her nostrils slightly distended, as she strove to control the surge of anger which ran through her at her mother-in-law's slight.

"I should say," Neil Murray was remarking slowly, "that the union must have been wholly successful, if this is the result." He drew Robin to him, and the child responded shyly. "What do *you* say, young man?"

Catherine Mailland's face was a study. She would not argue, however, and began to talk of the estate and their plans for Robin's future.

For the remainder of that painful half-hour Rhona remained in her corner by the door, and when Mrs. Mailland rang for tea, she went forward and lifted Robin with a feeling of immeasurable relief.

Gertrude rose from the chesterfield as they turned towards the door.

"Perhaps now that you have all finished baby-worshipping we can have some tea. I'm dying for mine, and I'm sure you are, Neil!"

She had forced a laugh into her voice, but she also managed to convey that the visitor must be bored to extinction with the parade.

Rhona permitted herself one glance at Murray as she went out, and he smiled kindly at her though without any sign of recognition.

Yet she knew that he had recognised her, and the fact that he had kept her secret before the others was no reason why she should change her mind about him, she reflected bitterly. Besides, what might he not say once she was out of the room? He was a friend of the family—an old friend. He had emphasised that fact himself when talking to Robin, and he was their solicitor into the bargain, and, as such, must safeguard their interests. He had done so before, so why not now?

Every limb seemed to be shaking as she made her way upstairs to prepare the nursery tea, and for once even the pleasure of being alone with her son was clouded over by the new fear which gripped her.

Wondering if the visitor had come over from Dulmore Lodge by car, she found herself more than once tensed, listening for the sound of a motor engine on the drive. When she did hear it she ran to the window of the day-nursery and looked out, her face pressed close against the cool pane.

The car came into view as it rounded the bend in the drive. It was a two-seater, and Neil Murray was at the wheel. By his side sat Gertrude Mailland. Of course—Neil Murray and Gertrude! Nurse Brodie had said . . . What *had* she said exactly? That Gertrude was keen on Neil Murray?

Her thoughts remained in chaos long after she knew Gertrude must have returned to the house, and when Enid Brodie made her appearance at seven o'clock she was kneeling on the nursery floor, gazing forlornly at Robin's scattered toys as if she were seeing them for the last time.

The expected reprimand did not fall from her senior's set lips, however, and Rhona rose hastily to her feet.

"You look tired, Nurse," she said. "Sit down and let me get you some tea."

"I am tired." Enid drew off her hat and gloves, and sank into the wicker chair beside the fire, resting her feet on the low nursing-stool. "No wonder!" she added. "Trotting half round Edinburgh after a fool of a woman who doesn't seem to know her own address. Putting Carlinghame Mansions in her advertisement instead of a number in the Corstorphine Road!"

Rhona looked frankly puzzled, and her companion laughed harshly.

"Haven't they told you?" she said, her mouth

twisting in an ugly expression. "I'm leaving Kindarroch at the end of the month."

"Because," Rhona asked, "of yesterday afternoon?"

"Not entirely." Enid Brodie kicked her shoes off with a vicious movement. "The official reason is my feet, of course. According to Mrs. Mailland I'm not fit for the job when they give me so much trouble, but I know damned well it's that sneaking little cat, Gertrude, who has put her spoke in my wheel with her everlasting tale-carrying! On the principle that constant dripping wears away a stone, she carried every little scrap of tittle-tattle to her mother, and her pleasant little insinuations did the rest."

Rhona felt genuinely sorry for the older woman.

"Are they getting another nurse?" she asked, her heart beating fast.

"No—not at the moment, anyway. That was why I thought you might have heard of my ignominious end!" Enid Brodie laughed more naturally now. "They feel that they can trust you to carry on yourself now, with one of the maids to help you." She looked up at Rhona frankly, her small eyes quite kind. "I'm not being spiteful," she said. "Your heart's evidently in the job and you'll probably survive. I'm getting too old for all this bickering, and I admit I haven't the patience I used to have. In a town job it might be different. I've had my own troubles these past few years, though, and perhaps it's just as well that I should be forced back to Edinburgh, where I have friends."

For some unaccountable reason Rhona found herself thinking of Doctor Inglis.

"I'm sorry," she said. "Isn't there anything to be done if—if you want to stay?"

"I don't want to stay. Not now," Enid Brodie declared. "I just couldn't stand Gertrude any longer. She's got her knife into me properly, and she'll never be content until I'm out." She rose and stood looking down at Rhona. "She probably thinks you'll be soft, and better suited to her purpose," she added. "You're keen on Robin, aren't you? Well, all I have to say to you is—watch Gertrude Mailland!"

CHAPTER FOUR

ENID BRODIE left Kindarroch on the last day of the month, and Rhona, watching the car disappearing in the direction of Kindarroch Junction, was conscious of a sudden feeling of apprehension which amounted almost to fear. With Nurse Brodie out of the house, she felt that she had lost a friend.

The thought of Neil Murray and the knowledge he held was never far from her mind, and the fear of dismissal began to grow from a cloud no bigger than a man's hand to a dark shadow which threatened her whole horizon.

How much this past month had meant to her she was only fully beginning to realise now when it appeared that all she had gained might be torn from her eager grasp at any moment. She had been happy —a word which she had thought had been banished from her world when she had made her decision and parted with her son. Neil Murray's decision! The swift thought struck at her with the force of a blow, and she set her teeth, determined to play for time, at least. Evidently he had not denounced her to Gertrude that afternoon of their meeting in the drawing-room, and he had not come to Kindarroch since. Mrs. Norris, the housekeeper, had remarked casually a day or two before that he had returned to Edinburgh where he was going into a Nursing Home for observation for a day or two.

Instinctively her one desire became to avoid the man who alone shared her secret, and the fact that

Murray had gone to Edinburgh for the time being was, at least, a respite. She turned away from the window, experiencing the exaltation of the knowledge that she was in complete charge of her son at last, that her word in his nursery was law, and her love might envelop him a little more closely than in the past.

Robin was having his after-dinner nap. Nurse Brodie had taken a silent farewell of him in the nursery as he lay in his cot so that she might not upset him. A parting otherwise might have been a tearful affair, for as soon as Nurse Brodie would appear in the nursery in hat and coat, Robin was well aware that it was time for his afternoon walk.

This afternoon, Rhona mused, her pulses racing with sheer elation, she would take him herself! This afternoon, and on many others, unless—unless Neil Murray came back to Dulmore Lodge!

Robin was just stirring out of his deep sleep when she went into the nursery, and she stood looking down at him with a smile hovering at her lips and an infinitely wistful expression in her dark eyes.

"Grant, just one moment, please!"

The harsh voice made her turn swiftly to find Gertrude Mailland approaching from the far end of the corridor.

"Yes, Miss Mailland?"

Gertrude ran her eyes over her critically from head to foot.

"Do you get into your uniform on your afternoon off?" she asked in some surprise.

For the first time Rhona remembered the date, and the fact that it should have been her free afternoon.

"I had forgotten," she confessed. "I—rather thought Mrs. Mailland would wish me to take another afternoon."

"Whatever for?" Gertrude was frowning slightly, but suddenly she laughed, a sound which grated unpleasantly on Rhona's ears. "Good heavens! do you mean because of Brodie's departure? That makes very little difference, I assure you. It is no tragedy!"

Rhona flushed.

"I don't mind forgoing my time off," she said, "until we can make more definite arrangements."

Gertrude produced a jade case and withdrew a cigarette, eyeing her narrowly.

"I don't think you need to worry about making arrangements, Grant," she said crisply. "I've told my mother that I will supervise the running of the nursery while she's away. Since she is going this afternoon to friends in Inverness for a few days, you can take my orders and have your free time as was originally intended. I will look after my nephew."

A cold shiver ran through Rhona, but she managed to crush back the impulse which wanted to refuse to leave Robin's side and said:

"Very well, Miss Mailland, just as you wish. I will get Robin ready for you."

"I'm taking him across to Colvend to see Lady Margaret," Gertrude intimated as she turned away and Rhona let the knowledge of her destination sweep the black fear from her heart. Why should she imagine that Gertrude Mailland would harm her nephew? It was surely a fantastic thought, yet she knew, even as she strove to banish it, that it still lurked at the back of her mind.

What, she wondered, would she do now to fill in her free and curiously empty afternoon?

Mrs. Norris, crossing the hall as she went downstairs, supplied the answer. Seeing Rhona hatless and in the blue coat which she had included in her luggage for leisure hours, she smiled at her encouragingly.

"Going out for the afternoon?"

"Yes." Rhona paused at the foot of the stairs. "What does one do here?" she asked.

"You might have caught the three o'clock 'bus into Perth," the housekeeper told her, "but you've let that go, and there's not another until after five, which is kind of late. There doesn't seem much else to do but go for a walk or a row on the loch."

"Oh," Rhona said, catching at the last possibility, "are we allowed to take a boat?"

"Provided you can handle one, and it isn't rough. The loch is only dangerous in squally weather."

"I used to be able to handle a boat quite well," Rhona returned. "An hour on the loch would be a change, and I suppose I may come back here for tea?"

"Certainly," Mrs. Norris nodded. "Come and have it with me."

"Oh—thank you."

"Fraser will give you the boat-house key," Mrs. Norris said as she turned towards her parlour. "I'll see you at half-past four. That gives you a nice hour's exercise."

The chauffeur supplied the key, but, as he was busy overhauling the car for the drive to Inverness, Rhona offered to get the boat out herself.

"You're sure you can manage?" he asked a little doubtfully, though obviously reluctant to leave his task. "There's a keel-run down to the loch."

"I'll be all right," Rhona assured him. "Don't trouble to come down."

There was a motor-boat and two dinghys in the boat-house, and she chose the smaller of the two light craft, found her oars and corresponding rowlocks, and pushed the boat down to the water without difficulty.

It was years since she had handled a boat, but the art, never really lost, came back to her as she dipped her oars, and she felt time slipping from her.

73

It was the fact that the sun had left the loch that brought her back to the realisation that the breeze which had merely wafted her gently across the surface of the water had stiffened to a strong wind. The loch had been whipped into little white-crested waves, and the whole scene had an angry appearance that was suddenly alarming.

Glancing quickly round, she saw that she was a long way from the Kindarroch shore, and facing her lay the little bay of Dulmore. The hills were dark and the coming storm lay over them threateningly, making them look cold and almost sinister as they brooded above the grey loch.

The first great splash of rain fell on the stern-seat as she was still wondering what to do. Apart from the certainty of a wetting, the loch was beginning to look dangerous and the wind was growing in strength and fury. Ahead, the sheltered bay of Dulmore lay like a sanctuary, but she dismissed the idea of taking refuge there.

Yet, Neil Murray was not at home. There was a little red-roofed shed nestling on the shore at the end of a grassy slope and she might be able to take shelter there and row back across the loch when the storm had spent itself.

Her face was flushed, her breath coming quickly, long before she reached the quiet water of the little bay. It was no great distance to the shore, but the final pull seemed to exhaust her completely, and she sat in the boat for a moment or two when she reached the stone jetty and drew breath. There was quite a lot of water in the bottom of the dinghy, the accumulation of rain and the waves which had been shipped over the side, and her light shoes were sodden and squelched dismally as she stepped ashore.

There was an iron ring set in the stonework of the jetty, and she tied her painter securely to it before she ran the remaining distance to the shed.

It was, as she had suspected, a boat-house and was larger than she had thought from the loch. It stretched back a considerable way into the shrubbery beyond and housed three boats—a white motor-launch, a small yacht of the Scottish Islands class and a dinghy similar to the one in which she had rowed across from Kindarroch. The yacht had evidently been laid up for some time, and neither of the other boats seemed to be in immediate use. The motor-launch had probably been the last out, since it was nearer the door, and it reminded her vividly of the incident of her flight from Neil Murray.

She rang out the hem of her dress where the water had collected and took off her damp shoes. It was cold in the boat-house and she began to shiver, wishing heartily that she had decided to spend the afternoon in the woods around Kindarroch or even chatting to Mrs. Norris in her comfortable parlour.

Thoughts of the housekeeper made her wonder what time it was. She had left her watch behind in the rush of getting Robin ready for Gertrude, and she had no idea how long it had taken her to row across the loch. The problem arose, too, of how she was to return if the wind did not abate. Certainly it showed little sign of doing so at the moment. It seemed to be whipping in vindictive fury round the shed and out across the water. Then another sound came to her ears, the sound of footsteps on the stone jetty coming round under the window towards the door.

She slipped her feet into her shoes and waited. Who could this be? Someone who had seen her from the house?

The door was pushed open and a stout figure in an oilskin coat and hat, and carrying a large golf umbrella, appeared in the aperture.

"I saw you from the house." The yellow sou'-wester drawn down over her eyes and the large, enveloping oilskin had obliterated sex, but the woman's voice sounded kindly and concerned. "You're fair soaked through," she went on. "Come away up to the house and let me see if I can get you some dry clothes."

Rhona hesitated.

"If the storm would clear——"

"It'll not clear for a bit," the woman declared, "and you're asking for pneumonia standing about in those wet things. Come along up to the house and let me get you something warm to drink."

Rhona submitted to the rough kindness and followed the woman from the boat-house up a narrow red blaize pathway between high shrubs towards Dulmore Lodge.

"Where have you come from?" her guide asked. "Kindarroch?"

"Yes," Rhona replied. "I'm the nurse there. This is my afternoon off, but I don't seem to have put my spare time to very good use troubling you like this," she added.

The woman had been walking slightly ahead of her, but now she paused and came back to share the umbrella.

"Oh, so you're the new nurse?" she asked interestedly. "I might have guessed that, of course. What happened to Brodie that they dismissed her? Did they find out that her novels were as great a handicap as her feet?"

Rhona had to smile at the blunt question, and looking up into the twinkling eyes of the older woman she realised that Enid Brodie had been sized up fairly accurately.

"She was fond of Robin all the same," she defended her late superior, "and she was nice once you got to know her."

The other grunted, whether in assent or disagreement it was hard to tell, and they reached the house in silence.

It was a long, low-built structure, with creeper-clad white walls and about it there was an open friendliness which struck the visitor to Dulmore Lodge even on such an unpropitious day. The torrential rain only seemed to have washed the terrace steps a little whiter, and the freshness of light walls and green creeper defied even the overcast heavens above them.

Rhona felt the welcome of it as if the old house had spoken to her, just as she had felt its call from the far side of the loch before she had learned who lived there.

"I'm Mr. Murray's housekeeper," the woman told her as they entered by a side passage and crossed a long hall made bright by panelled mirrors. "Come into my room and you can take off your wet clothes at once. One of the girls will draw you a hot bath and while you're in it I'll borrow some clothes for you. Your own are soaked through. We'll try to dry them for you in the kitchen."

Rhona thanked her and, when she was finally left alone in the bright little sitting-room where a fire of logs glowed in the small grate, she took off her sodden shoes with infinite relief. How kind the housekeeper was, she thought, and what trouble she was taking over a complete stranger!

When she came back from the bathroom she found the housekeeper waiting for her at the door of the sitting-room.

"I expect you'll be ready for a cup of tea now," she said, but to Rhona's surprise, she turned and led the way across the hall to a door on the far side. "We're to have tea here," she intimated, opening the door. "Mr. Neil saw you from the window and gave the order."

For a moment it seemed to Rhona as if her heart had stopped beating and then it raced madly on, and she found herself walking into the room with an assurance which belied the feelings within her.

Neil Murray rose slowly from his chair beside the fire, and she noticed that he was leaning more heavily than before on his stick and that his face looked pale and drawn beneath the coating of tan which still lingered on high cheek-bones and lean jaw. His grey eyes seemed even more keen and direct because his face was noticeably thinner.

"I'm sorry you've had this adventure," he said, as the housekeeper moved a chair near the fire for his unexpected guest. "It was fortunate Mrs. Trigg was here to fix you up."

"Very fortunate," Rhona acknowledged.

Mrs. Trigg poured out their tea, and Rhona was relieved to find that the housekeeper was to share the meal with them.

"Miss Grant tells me she's in charge at Kindarroch now," she remarked to Murray, when he handed over his teacup to be refilled. "I have been telling her I hope there will be no more changes for the bairn's sake. He's getting to an age when he'll be bewildered by too many new faces."

Rhona felt the colour ebbing from her cheeks as her host looked across the hearth at her.

"I don't think there need be any more changes," he said quite deliberately.

What did he mean? Was he suggesting that she might stay at Kindarroch? Could he mean to keep the knowledge he held to himself? The mere suggestion set every pulse in her body throbbing madly, yet she told herself that she was a fool to set her hopes so high.

A maid appeared at the door.

"Mrs. Trigg, please. There's a Miss Manson to see you. She says it's important."

The housekeeper rose.

"If you'll excuse me for a few minutes?"

Rhona sat very still after Mrs. Trigg had gone. She was alone now with the man who held her secret and, curiously enough, she was no longer afraid. In those few minutes before the housekeeper had been called away she had realised that she must be first to approach the subject of his future attitude. Her head went back in an almost defiant gesture as she faced him.

"Well," she said, "are you a believer in a lingering punishment?"

His dark brows drew together in a puzzled frown.

"I'm afraid I don't know what you mean," he said.

"You know who I am, though," Rhona put in quickly, her voice harsh with nervousness and painful recollection. "I am surprised that you have kept the knowledge to yourself so long. But perhaps you have a reason."

His mouth hardened.

"I have," he acknowledged.

"I thought so!" She gave a little derisive smile. "It might be interesting to hear your reason," she added with an effort.

"I don't know that you would call it a reason so much as a decision," he said slowly. "I am merely determined that never through me will you be hurt again."

"Again——?"

"Yes." He leaned towards her, his face grave, his eyes searching hers as if for something he failed to find on the surface. "I thought you would understand that first time we met at Kindarroch. I would give everything I possess to be able to take back the advice I offered you in Glasgow. I should never have presumed to influence your decision. I see my mistake now, when it is unfortunately too late in the day to do anything about it but beg your pardon."

"What can I do now?" she asked, appealing to him unconsciously.

"Nothing," he said swiftly. "You are committed to this thing and I am in it with you." He hesitated and then held out his hand. "May I ask that if ever you need a friend you will come to me?"

He saw her hesitation.

"It would be—the act of a friend to keep—my secret," she managed disjointedly at last.

His long fingers closed over hers.

"Thank you," he said. "And now"—he passed her the cup of tea which Mrs. Trigg had poured out for him—"do you mind if I have another cup?"

The housekeeper reappeared as Rhona passed his cup back to him.

"I've been on the telephone to Kindarroch to tell them not to worry and that you are all right," she intimated briskly. "I spoke to Mrs. Norris. She seemed quite put out to think that she hadn't been on the spot to look after you! She's going to put a fire on in your room for when you get back."

Rhona rose hastily to her feet.

"I wonder if my things are nearly dry, Mrs. Trigg?" she asked. "I should be getting back now that the rain has cleared."

The housekeeper crossed to the door.

"You'll go back in these things of Jessie's," she declared. "We'll send yours over to-morrow when they're fit to put on. Meanwhile I'll find you a coat. It is much colder outside now."

She hurried away, and Rhona turned back to her host.

"I'm causing such a lot of trouble," she said. "You have all been so kind."

"It's nothing," he returned almost brusquely be-

80

cause, in his attempt to rise, he had stumbled against his chair.

"May I help you?"

She crossed to his side and steadied him while he found his sticks, but somehow she could not refer to his injured foot, because she felt instinctively that the visit to Edinburgh had been a failure, and he was battling with a crushing disappointment.

"Bryden will take you back in the launch," he said, moving with difficulty towards the long window. "It won't take more than half an hour. It would be warmer by road, but unfortunately the car has gone back to Edinburgh this afternoon. My father brought me through this morning."

Mrs. Twigg came back with a coat and said that the rain had gone off, and Bryden had the launch ready at the jetty.

Rhona turned back to the tall figure at the window.

"I can only thank you—for all you have done," she said huskily.

The launch slid alongside the boat-house on the other side of the loch, and the Murrays' handyman jumped ashore and helped Rhona onto the wooden jetty.

"I'll run the dinghy into the boat-house for you, miss," he offered, untying the tow-rope which had brought the Kindarroch boat safely across the loch in their wake.

The side door was ajar as she approached the house, and she went in, still thinking of Murray and the problem he presented.

"Grant, I want you in here, please!"

It was Gertrude Mailland's voice, and it sounded full of suppressed fury. Rhona went towards the open door of the study with a sickening feeling of dismay. What now?

Gertrude was sitting at her mother's writing-table in the centre of the room, but she stood up immediately, probably because she considered that her height gave her an added advantage.

"So, you've been across to Dulmore Lodge this afternoon?" she questioned, permitting her pale eyes to rove over Rhona's strange attire. "What, may I ask, took you there?"

"An unexpected gale!" Rhona replied with a slight smile. "I went out in the boat and was caught on the far side of the loch. It was very wet, and I thought I might shelter in the boat-house at Dulmore until the rain went off and I could row back."

"How did Mrs. Trigg know you were there?" Gertrude asked. "She 'phoned through here to let us know you were safe."

"They—saw me from the house."

Rhona hesitated over her explanation, and immediately her interrogator pounced on the first halting word.

" 'They'?"

"Mrs. Trigg and Mr. Murray."

"Oh! Was old Mr. Murray at home? I thought he had gone to Edinburgh."

"It was Mr. Neil Murray who saw me from the window," Rhona told her. "Evidently he came home this morning!"

Gertrude Mailland's face underwent an alarming change at the information. From mild annoyance her expression switched to cold, dark fury.

"What right had you to go to the Lodge?" she demanded. "You know you have no right there when any of the family are at home."

Stung by the slight, Rhona said clearly:

"I hadn't the faintest idea Mr. Murray was at home. I thought the family were in Edinburgh—otherwise I would never have accepted the housekeeper's offer to go to the Lodge, I assure you."

Gertrude was looking at her closely, as if her words had opened a new train of thought in the alert mind behind the far-seeing, pale grey eyes.

"Very well, Grant." She sat down at the table again and drew a sheet of notepaper towards her. "You may go, but I think, in future, that excursions on the loch must be banned unless you are accompanied by someone more capable than yourself. Mr. Murray is too ill at present to be worried by such episodes. I, personally, will go over and apologise for the trouble you have caused this afternoon."

Rhona turned slowly and left the room. She felt strangely crushed in spirit by the interview, but she knew in her heart that it was not solely because of her sister-in-law's dictatorial attitude. What had cut deeper was, at the moment, difficult to say, but vaguely she knew that part of it was Gertrude's insinuation that there was more between herself and Neil Murray than just friendship.

Yet—stoutly her heart made answer—he had promised to keep her secret.

"Never through me," he had said, "will you be hurt again."

The words echoed reassuringly in her mind that night as she lay awake in her narrow bed in the little room at the end of the nursery suite listening to the last remnants of the storm blowing round the battered old tower. The deep soughing of the pines came to her like a complaining voice, and once or twice a gust swept rain fiercely against her window. She pictured the loch lying dark and turbulent under the night sky and the hills brooding over it, shrouded in mist. A door slammed somewhere in the quiet house and shortly afterwards a clock struck eleven. She lay listening subconsciously for the quarter-hour, but before it chimed another sound claimed her attention. She wondered, as she strained her ears for repetition of what had seemed a careful footfall, if it had not merely been a trick of her overactive imagination, and then it came again.

For a moment she could not place it. There should be nobody abroad in the nursery wing at this hour. In fact, since Enid Brodie's dismissal she had slept alone in this part of the house.

The sound came again, almost stealthily, and Rhona sat up in bed, her hand pressed against her throat where her heart seemed to be pounding madly. What was it? *Who* was it?

Suddenly she knew that the sounds had come from the tower, and at the conviction all personal nervousness was superceded by a fear for the child in the nursery farther along the passage.

Without a sound she swung her feet over the side of the bed and thrust them into her slippers, her ears strained to catch each movement, but the noise of the wind drowned the sounds which she had taken for footsteps. She felt for her dressing-gown with a feeling of hesitation. Probably her nerves had played her false, and she had let her imagination run riot.

She struggled into the warm wrapper in the darkness, however, and felt beneath the pillow for her torch. As her fingers closed upon it the distinct grating of a key in a lock reached her ears. She stiffened, her fingers tightening spasmodically round the torch.

She knew instinctively that the sound had come from the direction of the heavy oak door at the end of the nursery corridor, the forbidden doorway leading to the tower and the treacherous stair beyond.

And someone had tried to open it! Rhona knew that it was always locked from the inside, and the last time she had looked the heavy iron key had been in the keyhole.

Quivering from head to foot, yet goaded by a desperate anxiety, she sped along the short, dark corridor to the entrance to the tower.

Dimly she could see the dark arch of it against the white enamel of the corridor and she held her breath as she switched on her torch.

The blank face of the door met her with a sort of mocking disregard. There was nothing different about it, yet, so sure was her impression, that she bent forward and tried the handle. It turned in her grasp, but she pulled to no avail. The door was locked.

It had all been a mistake, a figment of her imagination, even a species of nightmare, perhaps! She turned away, relief struggling uppermost, and then, as if drawn back to look again, her gaze fell on the lock and she gave a little audible gasp of dismay. The key which had been there the day before was missing.

Desperately she tried the door again, but it resisted all her efforts to open it. It was locked and the key was gone. That was all there was to it. Someone had taken it away—for safety, probably. Had she, then, imagined the sounds on the stone stairway beyond her bedroom wall? It was a thick wall—four feet thick, Mrs. Norris had said that first afternoon—and stealthy footsteps would not be heard at all. Unless—the thought came to her with the suddenness of an inspiration—unless they were audible as the intruder passed close to the alcove which had been converted into a makeshift wardrobe for her clothes. At this point the wall would not be so thick, and the stair beyond was a stone one where footsteps would resound, however light.

She stood at the door for many minutes, listening intently, but there was no further sound. Even the wind seemed to have died with the coming of darkness and the rain had ceased its beating on the window panes. She turned along the corridor at last, reassured yet strangely perturbed in spirit. Was she becoming a prey to nerves? It was the last thing she could afford to let happen for Robin's sake as well as her own.

For a long time she lay awake, wondering if she should mention the incident to Gertrude Mailland in the morning and ask for the custody of the key, but some instinct which went even deeper than sober reason bade her wait.

In the cold light of morning the incident of the tower seemed vaguely theatrical. There was the door securely locked looking like any ordinary door, and though the key had quite definitely disappeared, Rhona felt that Gertrude Mailland would be quite justified in laughing at her wild statements.

Two days passed and, though the thought of the missing key disturbed her at intervals, she did not mention the matter to her sister-in-law. Mrs. Mailland was still away and intended to stay with her friends in Inverness for another week.

On the day following Rhona's adventure on the loch, Gertrude had gone across to Dulmore Lodge on her bicycle and had come back with a stern, set face and her eyes glinting dangerously.

"She's not had it all her own way at Dulmore," young Flora Macmillan had observed with a satisfied smile. "Someone's put her in her place, and I'd like to bet it was young Mr. Murray. He's the one for her, and, if she does marry him, it will do her good!"

Rhona had made no reply to the housemaid's remark, but she could not help wondering what had passed between these two at Dulmore Lodge. One fact emerged out of Gertrude's angry silence, however. Neil Murray had kept his word, and her secret was still her own.

The week-end passed uneventfully, but on the Monday morning Gertrude summoned Mrs. Norris, and launched a veritable campaign of complaints. The management of the kitchen was at fault, and

Rhona, hearing rumours of the general upheaval, fully expected her turn to come next.

She had just given Robin his breakfast when Flora came to say that Miss Mailland would like to see her immediately.

Smoothing her hair, Rhona crossed to the open window.

"How much longer do you intend to keep me waiting here, Grant?" Gertrude asked icily from the courtyard below. "I want you to come down here and look at this pram."

Rhona drew back and fastened the window behind her with an impatient jerk. As far as she was aware, the pram was in perfect condition, and Gertrude was merely trying to cause trouble. Deliberately she took her time descending the stairs and walked at a moderate pace round the house. When she reached the courtyard it was deserted, but almost immediately her sister-in-law's tall figure appeared round the end of the tower. Her breath was coming quickly as if she had been running. Her colour, too, was unusually high, but that might have been accounted for by her burst of temper.

"Where's Flora?" she demanded angrily.

"I'm afraid I couldn't say," Rhona replied calmly. "What is the matter with the pram, Miss Mailland?"

"The disgraceful condition of the wheels," Gertrude returned, but there was a queer hesitancy about her words as if she had only just discovered the fault.

At that moment Flora Macmillan came into view carrying the waterproof cover for the pram.

Before Gertrude could speak, however, the sound of running feet came to them across the courtyard and the maid whom Rhona had left in charge of Robin appeared, wild-eyed and breathless, from the direction of the side door. She addressed Rhona rather than Gertrude Mailland.

"I only left him for a minute," she cried. "Just for a minute, and I shut the nursery door. I don't know—*really* I don't know how he ever managed to get out."

Rhona turned to her, pale-lipped and trembling.

"What are you saying?" She gripped the shaking girl by the arm. "Agnes—do you mean—Robin?"

The girl seemed unable to reply for she nodded dumbly.

"What's this?" It was Gertrude's voice, and even in her sudden mental anguish Rhona detected a guarded expression in it, as if her sister-in-law feared to say too much. "What has happened to the child? Do you mean that he has—disappeared?"

Without waiting to hear the answer, Rhona turned and was racing back towards the side entrance as fast as her shaking limbs would carry her. Robin! Robin had gone! She found herself laughing and sobbing in the same breath. It was preposterous—utterly ridiculous! He had been there less than ten minutes before—there where she had left him in the day nursery, toddling round on his uncertain little legs. He could not have strayed far, even if the nursery door had been left open by mistake.

She reached the top of the stairs and went through the door into the white suite of rooms, still running, her heart pounding madly with her exertion, little beads of moisture standing out on her upper lip. The rooms were quiet, deadly quiet. No prattling voice, no noise, no laughter! She sought even in her own bedroom, and then she turned back along the corridor and found herself facing the door to the tower. Suddenly, she was turning the handle and the heavy door opened inwards at her touch.

She felt as if some great engulfing tide was washing over her, sweeping her onward and outward. Then, somewhere farther down the winding stone staircase rose a cry, a little, gurgling cry of delight and conquest. Robin had reached the bend in the stairway.

Rhona went forward. The place was like a vault and time seemed suspended and her hands were bruised against the rough sandstone of the walls as she plunged downwards.

She saw him standing at the foot of the first flight of steps on the little circular landing where the stone balustrade had given way, and a shriek of horror almost escaped her lips as he todded confidently towards the opening.

Could she reach him in time? If she called to him he might overbalance and fall. Her shaking limbs almost refused to carry her and then, with a smothered cry she pulled up, covering her face with her hands. When she looked again Robin had disappeared.

There was no sound for what seemed an eternity, and then a flood of light blazed upward. Someone had flung open the heavy outer door and the bottom half of the tower was full of sunshine. She went forward, almost falling down the last few dangerously worn steps to where Gertrude Mailland was stooping over Robin's inert little form.

"Don't touch him!" A feeling which embodied hatred and fear and terrible despair had forced the words from Rhona's shaking lips. "Don't touch him! It was you who did this—you who opened the door!"

She flung her challenge in her sister-in-law's pale face even as she brushed her aside and lifted her son into her arms, bearing him back up the treacherous stairway. That one look, however, had convinced her of Gertrude's guilt. The horror of it almost rooted her to the spot, but Robin's need was uppermost.

Other footsteps came running down the stairs from the landing above and Flora appeared, pale and dishevelled.

"Oh—the wee bairn! The wee bairn!"

Twice Rhona tried to speak and failed. Motioning the tearful Flora aside, she went past her to the night nursery where she laid her bundle tenderly in the cot.

Another figure came to her side and with a little quiver of relief she recognised Mrs. Norris.

"I've 'phoned for the doctor." The housekeeper's voice was low and steady, and it gave Rhona a measure of assurance. "It's his head, I think. We must do what we can until Doctor Jim gets here."

Rhona ran and brought hot water and towels and knelt down beside the cot, while Mrs. Norris bathed an ugly wound on the back of Robin's head. He was unconscious and his heart-beats seemed slow and uncertain under her nervous fingers.

"Doctor Inglis, Mrs. Norris."

The words seemed an answer to her silent prayer, and Rhona rose from her knees to confront James Inglis.

"Oh, Doctor Inglis, you'll save him, won't you?" she implored, caution and everything else thrown to the winds in this supreme moment of her son's need. "You must save him. You see—you see, he's all I've got to live for!"

She was conscious of the doctor looking at her closely, and knew that Mrs. Norris had closed the door on someone in the passage outside, but nothing seemed to matter but that pitifully still little figure in the cot.

It seemed hours before Robin moved, and Jim Inglis's face had turned almost as pale as her own.

"We may manage to pull him through," he said. "It will be a tough struggle, but I will do all I can."

He had spoken to Rhona more than to the housekeeper, and she clung to what small hope he offered, praying that his skill would save her child.

In the hours which followed, James Inglis did all he could. Never once did he leave Robin's side, and always Rhona was there like a grey, silent ghost, watching, waiting, praying for some sign that he would live. Inglis had debarred everyone from the nursery but Rhona and the housekeeper, and it was Mrs. Norris herself who went out and in with messages, who 'phoned Mrs. Mailland at Inverness, and carried out all the doctor's instructions.

Once, while she was out of the room, a light tap sounded on the door and Rhona rose unsteadily to her feet to open it. In the white passageway outside stood Hector Mailland, his kindly face grey with anxiety.

"How is he? I had to come?" he said almost apologetically.

"We don't know," she whispered.

He stood looking at her doubtfully for a moment and then quietly he asked:

"Would they let me see him, do you think?"

Unhesitatingly she opened the door wider and led the way back into the room. The young doctor turned from the bed as if in protest.

"It's—his grandfather," Rhona said simply, and James Inglis nodded and moved aside to make way for the old man.

Hector Mailland stooped over the cot in silence, and Rhona, watching him, realised that this must be a crushing blow to him. He had made little fuss, but probably Robin had meant more to him in his loneliness of spirit than any of them had ever dreamed. Before he turned away he touched the fair hair gently with those sensitive fingers which had brought healing to many an injured bird.

"Wee laddie!" he said softly, and went slowly from the room.

The day dragged to its close, and Rhona knew by the expression in Jim Inglis' eyes that there was little change to report. He remained with them as a matter of course, only leaving the nursery for meals or an occasional smoke. Rhona herself would accept no respite, and when Mrs. Norris suggested that she should rest for an hour she shrank nearer the cot and shook her head.

"You're awful fond of the bairn," the housekeeper observed.

As the hours of that silent, watchful night passed, Rhona began to look to Doctor Jim as if to a worker of miracles. In the dim light of the shaded bed-lamp his keen, thin face became the only real thing in the big white room. They sat together without speaking, and yet a strange bond seemed to have grown between them during those anxious hours of their shared vigil.

Even the longest night will pass, and Rhona, stiff and chilled in spite of the fire which Mrs. Norris had kindled in the room, saw James Inglis rise to his feet at last and draw aside the curtain to let in the dawn.

"He has survived the night," he said.

A woolly lamb lay forlornly on its side beside the cot, and she picked it up, kneeling with it in her arms. Then, as if some part of his spirit had responded to the miracle of another day, Robin stirred out of the death-like coma which had claimed him for so long.

Doctor Inglis was by his side in an instant.

"Speak to him—now," he commanded.

"Robin, here's Nanny!" she whispered, using the only name by which he knew her. "She's got the little white baa-lamb. See, Darling——!"

A flicker of recognition dawned in the dark eyes, and then the heavy lids fell once more.

Doctor Inglis permitted himself what might have been a sigh of relief, and, rising to his feet, motioned her to follow him to the window.

"I was afraid of compression following a fracture of the skull," he said quietly, speaking to her professionally, "but now I hope that we have merely to deal with a severe concussion. I know, nurse, that you will do all you can, and I will get you relief as soon as Mrs. Mailland returns. She will probably want to send to Edinburgh for a night nurse."

"Couldn't I manage?" Rhona implored, jealous of her charge and afraid in her anxiety to hand Robin over to a stranger. "I don't need much sleep, and Mrs. Norris would help."

He put a kindly hand on her arm.

"My dear girl, you're thoroughly worn out now, though you probably don't realise it. You seem to have been living on your nerves for a long period," he declared not unkindly. "I thought that the first time I met you and you don't want to crack up now that Robin needs you so much."

Rhona lowered her head so that the young physician would not see the agony reflected in her eyes.

"I'll leave you with him now for a few moments," he said. "Mrs. Norris will no doubt relieve you for a while after breakfast."

For a long time Rhona stood by the window where he had left her, facing the dawn. The sun had claimed the world for its own save in those dark crevices on the hillside where the rocks flung black shadows like scars on the green slopes, and she saw them like the dark and stony ways in life set among green pastures, one of which she was travelling now. Would there ever be green fields for her again? There seemed no answer in her empty heart and the pale heavens showed no sign.

A wind had risen and she saw the loch ruffled and grey at its passing, and far out beyond that grey belt, the calm waters of Dulmore bay. Faintly gleaming in the morning sunlight, she could see the strip of white sand, but the Lodge itself was hidden from view, and suddenly, bitterly, she was thinking of the sleeping owner of that quiet house and all he had contributed to the present state of affairs.

In her unhappy mind she found herself contrasting him with the man who had shared her vigil of the long night just behind her and thinking that Doctor Jim had fought to give her what Neil Murray had sought to take away.

At six o'clock Mrs. Norris came to relieve her.

"Try to sleep right away, my dear," the old housekeeper advised with something very tender in her voice.

Rhona went slowly from the room, and at the end of the corridor she came upon a pathetic figure in a navy-blue travelling coat with tear-reddened eyes and a pinched-looking white face whom she recognised as Agnes Halliday, the housemaid.

"Oh, Nurse," the girl began before Rhona could speak, "this is awful! I had to see you before I went. It wasn't my fault—word of honour, it wasn't! I wouldn't have left Master Robin, but she told me to go downstairs and find Flora and now—now she has dismissed me because she says it's all my fault."

Rhona, her lips tightly compressed, realised from this garbled statement that her sister-in-law had not been idle in the past few hours, but she knew that she could do very little about the girl's dismissal. It was, in all probability, Gertrude's way of silencing a dangerous witness.

"Don't worry, Agnes," she said kindly. "I—we all know you were not to blame."

"I'm not caring about being sent off without a reference," Agnes sobbed as Rhona led her away from the nursery wing. "I wouldn't have stayed here much longer, anyway. It's what *you* were thinking of me, Miss Grant, leaving little Robin—but she sent me downstairs and I had to obey her."

"Miss Gertrude sent you out of the nursery?"

"Yes. Oh, Miss Grant, I really did think she meant to stay with the baby."

"She came up by the tower—otherwise I would have met her on the stairs."

Rhona was never quite sure whether she had actually uttered the words for suddenly Gertrude Mailland was standing before them in the dim hall and Agnes had fled at sight of her.

Something seemed to snap in Rhona's brain and the floodgates of worry and anger were released.

"You dismissed Agnes Halliday because you were afraid she would tell the truth!" she accused blindly, careless of all that her outburst might mean for herself. "But I know. I know you opened the door to the tower and—and that was why Robin fell."

Instantly her arm was imprisoned in a grip of steel.

"Be quiet, you fool!" Gertrude commanded. "Do you want the entire household to hear?"

"I don't care who hears," Rhona declared wildly. "It's the truth—and you know it!"

"Be careful what you say!" Gertrude's pale eyes had narrowed, and her mouth was compressed into a thin, hard line that made her whole face look merciless and cruel. "You can't afford to talk like that to me, Grant," she continued maliciously. "I know too much about you."

Rhona stepped back a pace, freeing herself from the iron grip.

"I don't care what you know," she whispered. "I meant what I said and you know it is true. You are to blame," she repeated.

"You're making a mistake." Gertrude uttered the words calmly enough, relying on her forcefulness of character to break down Rhona's resistance. "You know perfectly well you're making a mistake and unless you drop this mad accusation I will go to my mother with the truth about your faked references."

Rhona shrank back, her pale lips quivering at the sudden revelation. Gertrude *knew*! How much? Her tired brain, wearied with her long vigil, seemed to be standing still and she could neither think nor reason.

"That staggers you!" Gertrude gloated, a derisive smile twisting her thin mouth. "I happened on the information in a rather interesting way, too. One might also call it a coincidence!"

Rhona waited in silence. It did not seem to matter now what happened; she was too tired, too worn out both mentally and physically, to care.

"A very close friend of mine in Edinburgh happens to have become engaged recently, and her future sister-in-law is a Mrs. Anthony Buchnall. Perhaps you recognise the name? It was there that you were supposed to have worked at one time." Gertrude spoke slowly and deliberately as if she derived a sort of sadistic pleasure from this cat-and-mouse game and was determined to play with her victim as long as it suited her purpose. "I was interested to meet Mrs. Buchnall and her two charming children the other day, but no doubt you will understand how much more interested I was to learn that *her* Nurse Grant had left her service to be married!"

Rhona roused herself with a great effort.

"You did not ask if I were married," she said.

"True!" Her tormentor was looking at her more closely now and Rhona had the swift impression that she was trying to trap her into some admission. "True," Gertrude repeated. "It struck me, though, Grant, that you must have a good deal to hide. Something unsavoury in your married life, shall we say?"

Rhona's cheeks flamed.

"There was nothing about my married life that I needed to hide. I am a widow."

There had been a dignity in her words which even her anger could not dispel, and Gertrude Mailland appeared nonplussed for the first time. She rallied quickly, however.

"That's as may be," she said, "but it doesn't detract from the fact that you obtained your job here under false pretences. Granted that your references *are* your own, you were deceiving my mother to a certain extent in using your maiden name and representing yourself as single."

She stood as if awaiting some reply, but Rhona made none. One fact had emerged to claim her attention to the exclusion of all else. Whatever Gertrude had found out, she had not yet discovered her true identity!

"I think you'll come to see reason, Grant," Gertrude was saying. "I'll give you a little time to think it over."

She walked away and Rhona went slowly up the stairs again, her steps dragging listlessly as she reached the nursery wing. Instantly, however, she was all alert. Mrs. Norris was coming from the night-nursery and her face was full of her deep concern. Rhona gripped her arm, not daring to speak.

"There's a change." The housekeeper shook her head and there were tears in her eyes. "I wish Mrs. Mailland would get here. Not that she could do more than we have done, but there's the responsibility and Doctor Jim's anxious. . . ."

Rhona heard no more. She was feeling her way blindly into the dim room which still smelt of pine-needles and the breath of the wind from the hills, and it seemed that all her life hung suspended within its four white walls.

James Inglis came slowly across the floor.

"We can't do anything more just now," he said kindly. "We must just wait. Nature will tell us—in an hour or so."

Robin looked as if he were sleeping; there was a little flush on his cheeks and his long lashes threw deep shadows under his eyes. She knelt down and suddenly terrible, tearless sobs were shaking her from head to foot.

James Inglis took her firmly by both hands and led her away to the fire.

"Come, my dear!" His voice was soft and gentle as a woman's. "You mustn't take it like this—not after the magnificent fight you put up last night." As he spoke his quick brain was working rapidly. "You're very tired. I asked you to lie down for an hour or two."

"I couldn't!" Rhona cried. "Don't you see, I can't rest while—while Robin's life hangs in the balance."

His keen eyes searched her face, and she was powerless to conceal the agony in her eyes.

"What is it?" he asked softly. "Can't you confide in me, Miss Grant? I'd do anything—all in my power to help you."

She looked up at him, and a deep wave of comfort swept over her, calming her spirit a little.

"I wish I could," she whispered hoarsely. "I only wish I could!"

He did not press for her confidence again. Instead, he said rather clumsily, because such emotion as he was experiencing now was new to him:

"Don't worry. It's not on the books that he's going to die—not if I can help it."

The door opened behind them and Rhona, expecting that it was the housekeeper, did not turn. She felt the young doctor's fingers tighten over hers.

"Ah, Mrs. Mailland!" he said, and released Rhona's trembling hands.

She turned to find Catherine Mailland's impersonal gaze fixed full upon her.

"Go down to my study, Grant," Mrs. Mailland commanded with deadly calm. "I will see you there when I have spoken to Doctor Inglis about my grandson."

The study was cold and cheerless. It was seldom used unless the mistress of the house was at home, and the fireplace looked to Rhona like a vast, empty heart.

When Mrs. Mailland came into the room she was still standing before the desk in the position which she had taken up when she had first entered. Her mother-in-law looked at her sharply.

"Grant," she began, "I'm not going to ask you for an explanation. I saw all I need to know up there in the nursery, and apart from being surprised and disappointed in Doctor Inglis, I am disappointed in you. Somehow, I imagined you were not the philandering kind."

Rhona did not even flinch at the implied accusation; she had passed beyond caring what the Maillands thought of her.

"However, one never really knows." Catherine Mailland sighed. "You will not be surprised to hear that I feel obliged to look for another nurse for my grandson."

"Oh—no!" The cry broke involuntarily from Rhona's lips. "Please let me stay—at least until—until——"

She could not go on. Catherine Mailland added briskly:

"You will work out your month's notice. Unfortunately, we can't very well do without you at the moment, or you would be dismissed on the spot. In future you will not be in the sickroom with Doctor Inglis unless there is a third person present."

A deep wave of intense mortification spread over Rhona's pale face, flushing it crimson, but the effort to defend herself or vindicate James Inglis seemed suddenly more than she could make. She sat down in the chair just behind her and buried her face in her hands.

There was a deep silence in which only the regular ticking of the clock on the mantelpiece seemed alive in the quiet room. Catherine Mailland spoke at last, not too unkindly.

"I must say, Grant, you were devoted to my grandson. I have heard of the way you stayed by his side after this appalling accident, and I really can't understand how you managed to let him stray out of your sight as you did."

Rhona did not denounce Gertrude. What was the use? Her sharp-witted enemy would have had plenty of time to construct a convincing alibi, and her denunciation would be treated as madness or viciousness following upon her own dismissal.

"Go to your room and try to get some rest," Mrs. Mailland ordered. "I will have a meal sent to you there. You may be needed again until I can get other professional help from Edinburgh."

Rhona stumbled to the door, a strange faintness blurring her vision, yet she managed to grope her way through the passage into the smaller hall, and found herself at last at the side door. She opened it automatically and went across the courtyard and out onto the drive, to be pulled up suddenly by the harsh grinding of a car's brakes.

"I might have run you over," Neil Murray said. "Rhona, what is it? Not Robin?"

The sharp edge of anxiety in his voice roused her out of her apathy.

"He is alive, but—but——"

"I only heard this morning," he said. "I came over right away. My God! this is awful for you!"

For her? He had thought of her first, not the Maillands! She found herself looking into his face, and all her antagonism was suddenly swept away in one great wave of understanding. This man knew better than anyone just what she was suffering. He knew and, somehow, she felt that he had come with the express intention of trying to see her.

"I wondered if I might see you," he said, confirming her thought. "Rhona, wouldn't it be better to tell them the truth?"

"No!" The cry came straight from her anguished heart. "No! They would send me away—even before the end of the month."

He thought that she was wrong, yet he made no effort to reverse her decision.

"I wonder if I can do anything?" he asked presently.

She shook her head.

"Doctor Inglis is doing all that is humanly possible just now," she said faintly.

"He's a good chap," he returned quietly.

Rhona turned back towards the side door.

"I mustn't be seen out here," she said.

He detained her for a moment longer, his hand on her sleeve.

"You will keep your promise to come to me if you need a friend?" he asked. "I know I'm not a lot of use," he added ruefully, glancing down at his stick, "but, like Inglis, I'll do all I can."

She could not answer him, but she looked into his eyes and nodded, turning away to the house with the feeling that her heart had become a little lighter. They were friends now, and instead of bitterness she knew a strange elation.

CHAPTER FIVE

IT WAS not until three days later that Doctor Inglis was able to say that his patient showed any sign of recovery and might, with careful nursing, eventually pull through.

And Rhona, during these long days and nights of anxious vigil, was constantly haunted by the fact that each day was bringing her inexorably nearer to the end of the month.

During that long nightmare of watching and waiting she had gone over the events of the tragic day of Robin's accident a thousand times, her senses reeling at the sure knowledge of Gertrude's treachery. Several times she had been on the point of confession to James Inglis, but they were seldom in the room alone together now, as Mrs. Mailland had decreed. Besides, she had no real proof against her sister-in-law.

Often she thought of Neil, wishing that he might come again so that she might thrust part of her burden of doubt and worry on his willing shoulders, but though he 'phoned Kindarroch for news of Robin twice daily, he did not visit the house.

On the fourth day Mrs. Norris practically forced her out of the nursery. A night nurse had arrived from Edinburgh that afternoon, a practical-looking, middle aged woman with sad grey eyes and a lined and kindly face, and Mrs. Norris declared that she would sit in the nursery until Nurse Pettigrew came on duty at nine o'clock.

"Off you go for an hour and get some colour into your cheeks!" she commanded, as Rhona would have refused. "You'll be no use to Robin or anyone else if you injure your own health, you know."

Perhaps it was true, Rhona thought, going slowly along the corridor to her own room. She invariably passed the door of the tower with averted eyes, though it had been boarded up now and the broken stairway barred with stout oak beams by Hector Mailland's orders.

Thinking of Molly Lang as she emerged later into the keen air that was like a sudden draught of wine after being confined so long indoors, she felt a sudden pang of utter loneliness, and the hills above Kindarroch were suddenly misty before her eyes. If only Molly were here! If only she had a friend, some woman in whom she could confide her grief and hopelessness!

She reached the head of the loch, and at the bend of the road Dulmore Lodge had come into view. Its sequestered peace seemed to be beckoning her, and almost against her will she walked on, her thoughts rushing ahead, grasping at the idea of Neil's friendship. He had asked her to come to him if ever she needed a friend, and—he alone knew her secret.

Almost desperate with worry and fear for the future, she could not think of what she was about to say to him. Her one thought was to reach him and let the remainder of the interview look after itself.

The white-pebbled drive to the house was flanked on either side by dense bushes through which, at intervals, a little path meandered down to the water's side. Presently the red roof of the boat-house came into view, and she hesitated, knowing herself near the Lodge.

As she stood there the sharp ring of a bicycle bell sounded behind her, and she looked round to find Gertrude Mailland cycling along the drive. She stopped less than a dozen yards away.

"What are you doing here, Grant?"

The question was rapped out in a tense undertone, and Rhona drew in a deep breath before she replied. It was the first time she had actually come face to face with Gertrude since she had accused her so madly of trying to injure Robin.

"I have come to see Mr. Murray."

"*You* have come to see Mr. Murray!" repeated

Gertrude, a sneer distorting her thin face. "Are you quite in your right senses, Grant?"

"I think so," Rhona returned, sudden anger banishing her nervousness. "My visit to Mr. Murray is entirely private."

"Indeed?" The pale eyes narrowed. "Well, I can tell you now that whatever your business with Neil Murray or however private you may consider it, I have no intention of permitting you to go to the Lodge this evening—or at any other time. I followed you from Kindarroch woods for that express purpose when I realised where your destination might be. You are still in our service, Grant, and I order you to return to Kindarroch at once."

Rhona stood her ground.

"There is just the possibility," she pointed out, "that I may refuse to go. I have been given permission to take an hour off, and I do not think you have any right to interfere with where I go in that hour."

"I have a right to see that my friends are not disturbed by my servants," Gertrude returned bitingly. "You are under notice, Grant," she added vindictively, "and if you are not very careful you will find yourself thrown out of Kindarroch long before Robin gets better—if he ever does get better!"

Rhona's high colour faded at the cruelty of the taunt.

"How can you say that!" she cried. "If I were you I would be praying every day for his recovery. It might lessen the terrible crime you committed——"

"So you're still on that theme?" Gertrude sneered. "You're a fool and you'll be recognised as one if ever you repeat your stupid accusations." Her mouth closed abruptly and her brows met in a dark line. "Was that the idea of trying to see Mr. Murray this evening?" she demanded. "Were you trying to carry your rotten suspicions to Neil, thinking he might offer you advice?" Suddenly she was laughing, a mad, derisive laugh. "What an idiot you are! As if Neil, of all people, would listen to a word against me! I may as well tell you that I am going to see him now at his expressed wish. He has something important to say to me."

If she had been suddenly struck a numbing physical blow, Rhona could not have appeared more stunned.

It seemed evident that Gertrude expected Neil's important announcement to be a proposal of marriage. Her smile, the intonation in her voice, the very words themselves, suggested that. Rhona turned away in the direction of the gates.

"Very well," she said faintly. "I will go back to Kindarroch."

"Just a minute, Grant!" Gertrude detained her. "You can ride back on my bicycle. Mr. Murray will probably want to drive me back himself, and it will save having to send someone for the cycle to-morrow."

Rhona took the machine without a word. Her eyes, as she left Dulmore Lodge behind, were bleak and detached, and in her breast arose a dreadful empty ache which threatened to engulf her completely.

She had counted so much on Neil's friendship, and now she knew that she could never appeal to him for either understanding or advice.

Gertrude Mailland watched her go with a malicious gleam of triumph in her pale eyes. What if she had reversed facts and said that Neil had invited her to Dulmore when, in truth, it had been she who had made the appointment by telephone less than an hour ago? She had disposed of someone of whom she had been secretly afraid and—the end would justify the means! She felt confident of the fact as she walked briskly along the drive, and across the lawn towards the front door.

Before she reached it, however, she became aware of a man's tall figure standing at the long windows of the study, and a wave of colour dyed her sallow cheeks as she recognised Murray, and knew that he must have been witness of that conversation at the bend of the drive.

Her unusually pleasant greeting struck Jean Trigg as slightly forced when the housekeeper showed her into the study.

"Miss Mailland, sir."

Neil turned from his vantage-point at the long window.

"Did Miss Grant wish to see someone here?" he asked without preliminary.

"Good heavens! No!" Gertrude laughed easily, though the pale eyes watched him closely. "She came over with me because I offered her the use of my bicycle this evening. She walked over and I shall walk back."

She was smiling openly into his face, and his eyes said frankly that he did not believe her.

"Look here, Gertrude," he challenged after the briefest of pauses, "what is the matter between you and—Molly Grant?"

A wave of uncontrollable anger swept through the woman who faced him across the desk.

"Molly——?" she cried passionately. "So it's true! You are as soft about her as that idiot, Jim Inglis! 'Doctor Inglis says this'! 'Doctor Inglis says that'! You should hear her, and then you would realise that you hadn't a look in!"

"I'm afraid," he said, and he could not keep an icy note from creeping into his voice, "you are trespassing a little, Gertrude, and perhaps you are even jumping to conclusions."

Gertrude saw her mistake. Indeed, from the moment she had given way to that uncontrollable surge of anger and allowed her jealousy of Rhona to fly to the surface in the presence of the man she had long since marked down as her own, she had regretted her hasty temper and unguarded words.

She smiled across at him, relaxing and taking out her cigarette-case.

"Really, Neil, that was quite a speech!" She lit a cigarette, tossing the spent match into the fire with a lazy movement, though the pale eyes beneath her half-lowered lids were watching him intently, every move he made, every fleeting expression which crossed his face. "You know I don't mean half I say when I fly into a rage. I didn't mean to accuse you of being a fool. All I thought was that I might offer a friendly warning." Her eyes swept up to his, and there was a little gleam of triumph in their depths. "You know she's married, of course?"

She saw his jaw tighten, and the gleam in her eyes deepened.

"I know she is a widow," he said deliberately.

Gertrude bit her lip.

"Of course! I expect she told you the sad, sad story, too! So young, isn't she? Left with nothing but the memory of her husband!"

"One must admire her for buckling to and getting a job. She may have someone to support, you know, a child, for instance," he suggested boldly.

Gertrude laughed.

"Oh, no! There's nothing like that. Probably that's why she has made such an idol of my nephew, especially in the presence of our impressionable Doctor Inglis! Nothing at all from her marriage to cling to—no chubby baby arms around her neck! You know how that line gets a certain type of man!" Gertrude puffed a series of perfect smoke rings into the air above her head. "She was probably drawing just that little bit of tragic glamour round herself when mother went up to the nursery the other day and found her in the doctor's arms!"

It was an exaggeration, but what did that matter? Gertrude Mailland was well past the stage where there was room for any twinge of conscience.

Neil had scarcely heard her last few words, though their implication had reached him in a vague way, adding the flavour of truth to her accusations.

"You wanted to see me?" he asked, in a business-like tone which prohibited all further reference to his feelings for Rhona.

"It's a very small matter, Neil," she said. "I thought you had better attend to it since you dealt with it in the first place. I want to sell out these Benderbury shares."

"Are you wise?" he asked, giving her his attention in the same cool way which secretly infuriated her. "They may become very valuable in time. Oil is worth having in that quarter, you know."

"I didn't come here to ask for advice," she flashed. "I came to tell you to sell for me just as soon as you can."

"Very well." He scribbled a note on his pad and closed it, a hint that the interview, also, was at an end. "I'll 'phone Jameson in the morning. They'll bring you in a good price, I should imagine."

His lips twitched as he saw her stub her half-smoked cigarette into the ash-tray with a vicious pressure which no doubt reflected her mood.

"I want to borrow a book, Neil," she said as she walked to the door, her voice amazingly under control. "Your father said I might get one from your library at any time."

"Certainly." Deliberately he stooped and pressed the bell on his desk. "You'll excuse me if I call Mrs. Trigg," he said. "I have promised to rest this leg of mine as much as possible, and I've been walking around on it rather a lot to-day."

Gertrude stood for a moment as if she were about to speak and then, her head held high, her pale eyes blazing, she reached the door as Jean Trigg opened it from the outside.

"Good-night, Gertrude," Neil said pleasantly. "I'll 'phone you when I have settled that business matter."

She did not answer him nor did she reply when the housekeeper remarked, quite innocently, that it was a pleasant evening for a walk.

Yet, she would have walked back to Kindarroch in a more pleasant frame of mind had she known just how accurately her barbed shafts had found their mark.

For a long while after she had left the Lodge, a book chosen at random under her arm, Neil Murray stood at the window of his study and gazed out upon the deserted drive. Deserted? No, it seemed to be haunted now by the vision of Rhona standing there and the thought which had flashed through his mind at sight of her. She had seemed to belong there—part of his dream of home!

His hands clenched suddenly round his sticks. What right had he to dream—a cripple, perhaps, for life? What had he to offer Rhona Mailland or any other woman, for that matter?

For one intensely bitter moment he thought of Jim Inglis, hating him, blindly cursing the fate which had sealed his lips while the doctor was free to proclaim his love for her at will.

Then, rising above this wholly human instinct, he saw that marriage with Inglis might be the complete solution of Rhona's problem. As the doctor's wife she would be near her son, and the threat of dismissal from the Kindarroch household would cease to hang like a sword of Damocles above her head. Of course, it would involve confession, but by that time she would be far beyond the Mailland reach.

His mouth twisted painfully as he sat down too abruptly and he let his sticks fall to the floor and covered his face with his hands. If only he had been fit—fit to give her the confidence and render her the services which James Inglis was probably doing so willingly! He had offered her his friendship, but what real good was an inactive friendship to her now?

Yet, as he sat on, listening subconciously to the ticking of the clock behind him, he wondered if she would come to him in a crisis.

James Inglis closed the door of the night-nursery behind him, but instead of walking towards the stairs he turned to the right and went swiftly along the white passage until his progress was barred by the arched door of the tower. He stood confronting this barrier thoughtfully, his brows drawn together in a scowl, and then he bent swiftly and tried the handle. The door was locked. Barricaded now, he thought, after the damage had been done—or almost done! There were a few facts about this accident, not strictly medical facts, which puzzled him and his sharp brain, accustomed to probe deep beneath the surface in order to arrive at a correct diagnosis of each case, found some things which, to say the least of them, were distinctly interesting.

He turned from the door and walked slowly down the stairs. Mrs. Norris came hurrying from her parlour.

"You didn't ring, Doctor?"

"No," he said, smiling at her in the way she had always found irresistible. "I thought I could let myself out."

"How is he—Master Robin?" she enquired anxiously.

"A great deal better, I am glad to say," he returned, "but he must have complete rest and quiet for a few days. Then, I have no doubt, we might get him out for an hour or two if this fine weather continues." He pulled on his gloves and turned at the door to face her. "Mrs. Norris, can you tell me where I will find Nurse Grant?" he asked abruptly.

Mildred Norris was well aware of the ban put on these two by her mistress, but she was a sympathetic soul and kind-hearted, and she had not grown old enough or disillusioned enough to forget her own youthful romance.

"She went out half an hour ago," she said. "You'll probably find her down by the loch."

"Thanks." He smiled at her again. "Look after Robin till she gets back, Mrs. Norris," he added unexpectedly.

It did not take him long to find Rhona. She was seated on a spur of rock screened from the house by a group of pines, and the book she had brought with her still lay unopened by her side. When he came within hailing distance he called her name.

"Miss Grant!"

She turned immediately and jumped to her feet. "Is there anything wrong? Robin——?"

Swiftly he reassured her.

"No, he's all right." He came up to where she stood. "Sit down again, won't you? I wouldn't have called you if I had thought it was going to startle you."

She sat down with a little sigh.

"I'm afraid I'm getting morbid these days," she said. "Everything seems to presage bad news."

"You're very fond of Robin," he remarked, experiencing once more that strange feeling of some hidden reason for her devotion to the child.

She inclined her head, but did not speak, and for a moment or two he sat looking out across the blue waters of the loch wrestling with a decision which he had been on the point of making several times in the past few days. Then, quite suddenly, he made it.

"Miss Grant," he said, "I'm rather worried over the true origin of this accident. It strikes me that there was more than carelessness behind that opened door."

Rhona stiffened.

"Please," she whispered, "need we discuss it?"

"I think we must," he said decisively. "Will you answer my questions?"

"If I can."

"They are about Miss Mailland." He was watching her closely. "Perhaps you are not surprised?"

Rhona moistened her lips, but no words would come.

"You said, when we were discussing the accident," Inglis went on, "that she called you downstairs. Had she been in the nursery wing before that —say, within half an hour?"

"No——"

"She was at the side door, then, when you came down?"

"No."

He looked strangely elated.

"Miss Grant," he said, bending over her, "how long would it take you to go downstairs? Did you hurry?"

"No. Oh, please!" she cried suddenly, bewildered by this catechism, "what does it matter now? Robin is going to get well—you said that this morning, didn't you? Must we go into all this? Nothing really matters if he gets better."

"Do you believe that?" he asked, his lips tightening. "I am not of the same opinion. I think that all crimes should be atoned for—one way or another."

"A person's own guilty conscience must be punishment enough," she faltered.

"Not if they haven't got a conscience," he returned harshly. "I tell you honestly, Nurse, that I believe we are dealing with a person who might, in less fortunate circumstances of birth and upbringing, have developed into a dangerous criminal! Gertrude

Mailland doesn't know the meaning of the word conscience. I believe," he added distinctly, "that, for some fiendish reason best known to herself, she unlocked the door of the tower in a deliberate attempt to kill her nephew."

The effect of his words on his listener was so drastic that he caught both her hands in his.

"Look here, I didn't mean to upset you like this! I hadn't the faintest idea you—felt so deeply about it."

Rhona was quivering from head to foot, her face ashen.

"It has given me a shock," she confessed, "you—seeing so plainly——"

"Then, you know it to be true?"

She nodded. What use to deny it? She felt incapable of the effort.

"My theory is that she must have called you down knowing it would take—say, four or five minutes for you to reach the side door," he calculated shrewdly. "Then she went up through the tower—a matter of a few seconds, if she hurried—dismissed the housemaid, and returned by the way she had come, leaving the doors open behind her."

Rhona covered her face with her hands.

"What can we do about it?" she gasped. "We have no proof."

"No." Reluctantly he made the admission. "As you say, we have no proof."

A silence fell between them, and their thoughts drifted apart. Rhona's were still on the revelation that someone else shared her suspicions about Gertrude, and it seemed to magnify Robin's danger a thousandfold, and make her own position at Kindarroch unendurable. It was impossible to go on like this, but what else was there for her to do? Tell the Maillands the truth? She had thought round that solution so many times that her mind had become a blank, and she invariably arrived at the same pitiful conclusion. If the Maillands discovered her duplicity they would surely feel that their former opinion of her was more than justified, and they would put every conceivable obstacle in the way of her seeing Robin in the future. It was a vicious circle no matter how she looked at it, and her tired brain reeled and could no longer reason.

James Inglis, on the other hand, had dismissed the problem of Gertrude from his mind for the moment, and given full rein to a desire which he had recognised before and kept strictly to himself. He looked down at his companion and the hopelessness in Rhona's face stirred something fiercely protective within him.

"Look here—Molly," he began, "are you really happy at Kindarroch?"

"I—am as happy at Kindarroch as I could possibly be anywhere." Suddenly her lips were trembling. "But I am leaving at the end of the month."

"Leaving?" he asked incredulously, and a queer look of disappointment appeared in his frank eyes. "Somehow," he declared, "I didn't think you would leave like that."

"I was dismissed," she told him frankly.

He sat upright.

"Dismissed in the middle of the boy's illness—right in the thick of a crisis? How like the Maillands! May I ask why?"

"Mrs. Mailland thought I was not attending to my duties strictly enough."

"You!" He laughed. "Heavens! What does she want? I went out of my way to tell her that Robin's mother couldn't have shown more concern and affection or served him so untiringly as you did——"

He broke off abruptly as Rhona gave a little strangled cry, and instantly and rather awkwardly his arms went round her and drew her head onto his shoulder.

"Molly," he said kindly, "what's troubling you, child? I want to know, and then I may be able to help you." There was no response, only the sound of Rhona's swift breathing as she struggled with her emotion and the rustling of the thick foliage above them as a wind began to stir in the pines. "If you're afraid that you may be without a job—don't worry. I think that I might be able to help you in that direction."

She raised her head, looking at him directly, and she did not care any longer that this man could see the marks of her grief.

"You are always so kind to me," she said. "I couldn't ask you to do any more for me—even if it were possible. My only hope is that I haven't injured you in any way—with Mrs. Mailland, I mean."

"I'd like to strangle that woman!" he declared savagely. "Molly—I had no idea that you had to stand the racket for that incident in the nursery when she came in and saw us hand in hand. Lord!" he exclaimed, "it makes me wild how some folks are everlastingly jumping to conclusions, and generally it's the wrong ones they make the most song about." He smiled crookedly. "So that was the reason for the lady's frigid reception of me afterwards! I was supposed to have committed a breach of professional etiquette—and in *her* house, too! Lamentable!"

"She is very strict," Rhona said automatically, "and she would not stand for anything like that."

"Why didn't you deny the allegation?" he asked. "You know I would have backed you up."

"I was too upset. I wasn't thinking of myself or the future at all—only of Robin."

Her reply puzzled him and the strained look in her eyes brought back that vague feeling which had troubled him before.

Then, he was saying quickly, disjointedly:

"If she did think that, what does it matter? Molly"—he caught her hands, holding them close—"I've been thinking such a lot about you lately. I—we've worked together under conditions that bring a man and woman very near—fighting to save the life of a child, and we've won through—together. Couldn't it be that way always, my dear? I—what I'm asking is—will you marry me?"

The words of his proposal were so utterly unexpected that Rhona gazed at him in complete bewilderment for a moment and then her eyes filled with a deep and singularly tender emotion. This was the man who had saved her son's life, who had given her back her child and all that life meant to her, and he had told her that he loved her. It seemed pathetic that he should be pleading with her for love, an emotion which she knew instinctively that she could never feel for him.

And yet, having loved once, was she ever likely to love again in the way she had accepted the meaning of the word? Wasn't respect and friendship enough, and added to these the fact that her marriage to James Inglis would ensure that she would remain near Robin? Yes, that would indeed be worth all the other considerations put together. And what of the doctor's side of the bargain? What had she to offer him in place of love? Trust, faithfulness, a devotion strong because of the debt she owed him.

Suddenly the thought of Neil Murray blazed across her mind, like a meteor across some dark sky, paling all else into insignificance. She sat stunned and shaken and curiously incapable of thought.

"Molly," Inglis said softly at last, "have you no answer for me?"

She seemed to come out of some far dream-world which shattered even as she came back to earth. If she loved Neil it was a one-sided affair. She was nothing to him. He knew the truth about her, and he had generously promised to stand by her if trouble came—but that was all.

"We could be happy together, you and I," the young doctor was saying. "I feel that I have known you for a very long while."

"But you don't know the very first thing about me," she confessed, "otherwise you would not be asking me to marry you."

He smiled steadily into her distressed eyes, his own calm and sure.

"I know all I want to know—all I will ever need to know," he declared. "We were not together on the night of the crisis without me being able to see right down into your heart."

Rhona drew in a swift breath.

"Then—you know that I am Robin's mother?"

Immediately she had uttered her confession she saw that he had not known, but she was not sorry that she had made it.

"I had no idea," he said, "but now I see—many things, and I'm not really surprised——"

She knew that he was hesitating over her name.

"I am Rhona Mailland," she said. "And—now you know what I have done."

"In order to be near your son!" he said gently. "Oh, my dear! how you must have suffered, and I, like a blundering fool, saved you nothing."

"You did not know."

He paused before the truth of her words, and his quick brain examined the situation from this new angle. It made very little real difference, he concluded. He still wanted her to marry him. Her so-called confession did not alter that fact in any way. There was the problem of her son, of course, and what they should do about the Maillands, but all these things could wait. What he felt was more imperative at the moment was the answer which every leaping pulse in his body demanded.

"Rhona," he said, using this new name awkwardly because it implied so much, "could you care for me in time?"

She tried to meet his eyes and failed.

"I—don't know," she whispered. "I owe you so much——"

"I am not asking for return," he said quickly, "not in that way. I did my duty as a medical man, that was all. What I want to know is—have I a chance of making you happy after we straighten out some of this tangle? If you care for me even a little, the other thing might come along in time."

"We must wait till Robin is well again," she said, knowing it a plea for time. "I can't think of anything else just now—I can't make any decisions. . . ."

He held her hands to his lips and kissed them tenderly, a gesture which looked strangely foreign in contrast with his square British build and the unruly red hair and candid grey-green eyes.

"I will wait," he said huskily. "I feel that you have given me half an answer, Rhona."

She did not think to question his statement, but she felt that she had drifted into a haven where friendship and the protective affection which this man offered so selflessly might one day compensate for love.

There was relief, too, in the thought that James Inglis knew the truth at last.

The doctor walked with her to the edge of the shrubbery, and there he left her with an encouraging smile and a last word of advice about Robin.

"See that he sleeps as much as possible, Rhona. That's nature's surest cure."

His car was parked at the main doorway, and he went round the side of the house and drove slowly away. At the end of the drive he was about to turn towards the village when he saw a familiar car approaching from the opposite direction. Immediately he applied his brakes and jumped out.

"Hullo, Neil! Feeling slightly more fit to-day?" he enquired as the other man extended a hand in greeting. "How's the leg?"

"A good deal better, as a matter of fact, though still gammy!" Neil Murray's white teeth flashed in a smile behind which lurked crushing disappointment and the hint of bitterness. "I feel half inclined to have it off and get a wooden one! At least, it would leave me in peace!"

"Nonsense, man! Everything takes time, you know. What did the Edinburgh johnny say?"

"In a year—or even six months, if I'm lucky—I'll be walking with a limp and nothing else to show for it!"

"Well, it's not so bad at that," Inglis told him with the bantering smile of old and tried friendship. "You don't have to look for a job, anyway. You can still swindle people even though you walk with a limp!"

A dull flush spread over Neil's face, and he looked away from the shrewd green eyes watching him with frank interest.

"I did something like that not so long ago," he said, as if the confession had been forced from him, "but I guess I've had my lesson." He looked up at the doctor with a queer smile. "Ever felt that you wanted something more than the whole round world put together, Inglis, and then realised that you hadn't the right to ask for it?"

"Once," James Inglis confessed, "but it's always best to ask, you know, just in case it might come off." He considered the man in the car closely, and suddenly he found himself making a confession. "I've been doing a bit of asking myself, lately," he said. "I didn't think I had the ghost of a chance with her, but half a promise is better than none, I guess."

Neil smiled, a queer, gripping sensation rising in his throat.

"You're not thinking of getting married, Jim, surely?" he asked. "I thought you were a confirmed bachelor the last time we held forth on the subject."

"I was—more or less," the doctor agreed, "but that was before I met Rhona."

Neil looked up swiftly and then as swiftly away. It seemed that something had died within him.

"You know—about Rhona, then?"

Their eyes met and held; there was surprise in Jim Inglis's, too.

"Yes, but I rather thought I was the first person she had confided in around these parts," he remarked.

"I met her long before she decided to come here as Nurse Grant," Neil confessed quietly. "In fact, I was instrumental in putting the Mailland's proposition to her in the first place—a fact which, I am afraid, she has never quite forgotten."

"I can understand her point of view," the doctor returned. "She must have been almost beside herself when she realised that she had parted with the boy— virtually for good, for I'm quite sure the old lady had no intention of having her to Kindarroch to see the child even once a year."

"I think Rhona knew that."

"Did she sign anything?" Jim Inglis asked reflectively. "I mean, was there any document to say that she had handed the boy over and agreed to waive her right to see him?"

"No," Neil replied slowly, "fortunately there was not."

It was on the tip of the doctor's tongue to speak about Gertrude to this man he had known from boyhood, but he was not quite sure how the land lay in that direction. Rumour had it that Gertrude was infatuated by Neil, and he had heard, at various bedsides where the patient was still able to take a lively

120

interest in village gossip, that there would be an engagement in that direction shortly. All the same, from his intimate knowledge of Neil Murray, he strongly doubted it. Quite possibly it was Gertrude who was making the running. Anyway, he could well imagine it!

"This accident has been a deplorable business," Neil said gravely. "It's really a wonder Rhona did not give herself away completely."

"Yes, it has all been a terrible strain on her nerves. The boy's recovery has been a miracle, and she has been living through a veritable hell of worry. That's why I want to get her out of it as soon as possible."

Neil bent over the steering-wheel.

"Look here, Jim, wouldn't the best way be to make a clean breast of everything now?" he suggested. "We can stand by Rhona, and it would have to come out in any case, if—if you marry."

"Of course, but then I would have the *right* to protect her."

"You'll straighten it out sometime, I guess," Neil said, and the doctor let him drive on.

Neil drove away. His mind was a blank, and yet a thousand conflicting thoughts seemed clamouring to enter it. He was almost home before he remembered that he had been going to the village to send off a business telegram.

When he turned in at his own drive he was surprised and just a little irritated to find Gertrude Mailland walking ahead of him, her shoulders hunched forward as if some burden weighed them down.

She heard the engine, and turned as he slowed up.

"Oh, hullo, Neil!" There was something evasive in the way she looked at him. "I thought I would call in to see if you had any word for me about these securities of mine."

He raised his brows.

"You haven't given me a great deal of time," he pointed out quite frankly.

"Haven't I? I'm sorry."

He felt that her mind was not on their conversation, that the shares she had asked him to sell for her were not the real object of her visit to Dulmore.

"Are you coming up to the house?" he was forced to ask.

"If I may?"

He opened the door of the car and she got in beside him.

"I've just been talking to Jim Inglis," he remarked. "He seems to think that your nephew has turned the corner."

Gertrude looked round at him swiftly.

"What did he say?"

"Just that the boy's recovery was a miracle, more or less."

There was a deep silence and Neil fancied that his companion was calculating something in that shrewd brain of hers. At last she asked, her voice holding a rather strained note of indignation:

"I suppose there isn't any form of punishment for causing such an accident?"

"Any legal form, do you mean?" he asked, puzzled by the question.

"Yes. I mean, carelessness—wilful negligence," she said. "Servants should be brought to account, I think, when something like that happens."

He helped her out of the car at the front door before replying.

"I'm afraid you'd have trouble in proving such a statement, though it does look as if someone had been careless," he said. "The only punishable offence would be attempted murder."

Gertrude's hands clenched slowly by her sides.

"Surely nobody would suspect that?" she said coolly.

Some quality about her reply made Neil turn to look at her, and she met his scrutiny with something like challenge in her eyes, stirring a queer doubt in his active brain. What were these questions leading to? He was quite well aware that Gertrude rarely wasted her time in idle speculation. There must be some reason for her probing into the subject of punishable offences, some deep reason affecting herself.

The issue worried him as they sat over the tea he ordered, and his guest launched into conversation about the gardens and the fishing in the loch.

"I'm fond of Kindarroch, Neil," she observed, and the remark brought him back to the present because there seemed to be something vital in it for him. "I would not like to leave it."

"You're not thinking of leaving?" he asked.

"I don't know." She made the reply guardedly. "Sometimes I think it will be very hard for me to stay on when—my nephew grows up. He inherits everything, you know."

She could not keep the venom from her tone nor the glint of hatred from her eyes, and suddenly it seemed to Neil Murray that his brain had cleared. Here, then was reason enough for her first seemingly pointed questions! Details in an almost complete chain of evidence presented themselves one by one and he stood aghast at the truth they revealed. He could not doubt for an instant that Gertrude Mailland had planned murder in an overmastering wave of jealousy and hatred. Long ago he had stumbled upon her almost insane desire for power, and he knew that the prospect of one day owning Kindarroch had represented power to her. She had seen herself as the Mailland of Kindarroch if anything had happened to her brother, and the fact that Alan had left a son to inherit the name and all that went with it had been a bitter blow.

But not, evidently, a crushing blow. From the moment the boy had come to Kindarroch Neil could visualise her scheming for his removal and the only, final way had been—this.

He was appalled by the revelation, but he could not doubt it, and in that moment he felt capable of murder himself.

"Alan's son has a right to inherit everything," he heard himself saying coldly, "and no one can take it from him."

A dark flush spread over her sallow cheeks.

"You seem to have very little sympathy for me, Neil," she accused. "But for that child, Kindarroch would have been mine."

"I have no sympathy for you at all," he returned, swift anger sweeping all discretion from him, "and the sooner you put the idea that you have a 'right' to Kindarroch out of your mind, the better. It might prove dangerous."

"What do you mean?" she flashed.

He rose slowly to his feet, leaning heavily on his sticks, but there was a commanding quality about him in spite of his injury which even Gertrude recognised.

"I think you know what I mean," he said. "I would advise you to keep—within the law in future."

Anger flamed in her pale eyes, and her baffled rage was terrible to see.

"How dare you speak to me like this!" she cried. "You have no right. You know nothing——"

"Only what you have told me, Gertrude," he said quietly, moving towards the door.

She was there before him, however, barring his exit.

"What are you going to do?"

"Nothing," he said, "at the moment."

She drew back, a look of relief spreading over her flushed face.

"How—theatrical we are becoming!" She took out a cigarette, but her fingers were trembling as she fumbled with her lighter. "You'd almost think I had to answer to you for my actions."

"I sincerely hope you won't have to do that," he said frigidly. "I would be a stern judge."

. She puffed a cloud of smoke in his direction, mastering her emotions with a supreme effort.

"Don't be silly, Neil!" she said lightly. "Your accident seems to have made you very morbid!"

"It has given me time to see a great deal that I might have missed in the ordinary way," he told her.

She glanced at him sharply, but she still managed to smile as if his words held no meaning for her.

Mrs. Trigg showed her out, and when the housekeeper came back into the room she found her young master standing at the mantelpiece leaning on it with one arm, his brows drawn together in a frown as he gazed down into the heart of the fire.

"I thought it was Nurse Grant that was with you at first," she observed, seeing him start at the mention of the name she had guessed was very near his heart. "She's a nice lass, and one I could be right fond of," she went on with the privileged candour of an old and valued servant. "She's quite different from the ordinary run o' nursemaids."

"Yes, quite different, Mrs. Trigg."

The housekeeper sat down on the chair Gertrude had vacated.

"You're kind of fond o' her," she said softly. "Is that the trouble?"

He roused himself, smiling down at her.

"It would be the trouble if she was not 'kind of fond' of someone else," he admitted.

"But how do you know she is?" The supposition

was ridiculous in Jean Trigg's faithful eyes. "Have you asked her?"

He shook his head.

"Why not?" demanded the ruthless old inquisitor. "You never know what's in a lassie's heart till you've asked."

"True, but sometimes the fact remains that one has no right to ask, Mrs. Trigg."

"No right? What makes you say that?"

"Look at me!" He turned on her almost fiercely. "A man who will probably never walk without the aid of a stick, and then ask yourself what right I have to ask any girl to tie herself to me for life!"

There was a deep silence in which a single, slow tear coursed down the brown, wrinkled face of the woman in the chair.

"You were aye that proud, Master Neil," she said brokenly. "I would sit in a wheel-chair for the rest o' my life mysel' if I could gie ye back the full use o' your limbs, for I'm sure the lassie loves ye. Ay, some-how, I'm sure!"

Neil turned sharply away. What he called Jean Trigg's absurd faithfulness had pierced him to the heart, and he could find nothing to say to her in reply.

CHAPTER SIX

IT seemed to Rhona that the days of the month were running out like sand through an hour-glass and her heart grew as heavy as lead as she contemplated the last ten days of her sojourn at Kindarroch.

The night nurse had been called away to a more urgent case, and Rhona had suggested that she should sleep in what had been Enid Brodie's parlour so that she might be next door to the nursery. Mrs. Mailland had readily agreed.

James Inglis stopped coming twice a day and paid his visit now only in the mornings. Robin, he said, could be wheeled out in his pram, but on no account was he to be allowed to stand on his feet for several weeks to come.

Invariably at this point the shattering thought of her dismissal would rush in upon her, and she would experience a sensation of panic. What would happen when she had gone?

It was in these moments that she thought again of James Inglis's proposal of marriage. It seemed one way out of her troubles, for, if the Maillands insisted on Robin being brought up at Kindarroch in later years she knew that the doctor would ask for his custody now.

The morning when she first carried Robin down the stairs and laid him in his pram was like the beginning of a new era to her. James Inglis had given his consent to the walk ten minutes earlier, and then gone to report her grandson's favourable progress to Catherine Mailland, and as Rhona walked slowly and carefully along the drive towards the main gates, he caught up with her.

"You look as if someone has handed you the world on a silver salver," he greeted her.

"Someone has!" She turned to smile at him. "*You* have, Jim—giving Robin back to me."

"I'd feel a lot happier if I could give him back to you in all earnest," he told her gravely. "I don't think this state of affairs can go on much longer. We must do something, Rhona. Certainly we must do something about Gertrude."

"What can we do?" she asked with a little shiver. "You admitted yourself that we have no proof."

"I wish we hadn't let that housemaid go," he said. "Of course, Gertrude got in first there, didn't she? I must admit she was slick in removing any damaging evidence."

"Perhaps she has learned her lesson," Rhona suggested. "She never comes to the nursery now. She may even be regretting what she did."

"Don't you believe it——"

He broke off abruptly, seeing the look of distress his words had brought to her eyes.

"Surely she would never dare to harm him again?" she said pleadingly.

"If she did, I'd have not the slightest compunction in certifying her insane," he declared. "No, don't worry. No further harm will come to the boy if I can help it, and you've a staunch ally in Neil Murray, you know," he added. "If ever you need advice and I am not there to give it to you, go to Neil."

"I feel that I do—so little for all this friendship," she said huskily.

"Friendship doesn't look for return, my dear," Jim remarked kindly.

When he had gone she wheeled Robin down the white-sanded road where the leafless branches of the beeches stretched gaunt to the sky, and the grey water of the loch glimmered through the dark boles of the larches like a pale, sad face peering out through prison bars. Birds hopping about among the dead leaves of the undergrowth brought Hector Mailland vividly to mind, and she had an almost overwhelming desire to tell Robin's grandfather the truth, for he, at least, would understand the motive which had brought her under an assumed name to live in his house. Yet, by doing so, would she not be exposing him to the wrath of his wife and daughter?

She turned the pram before she came to the head of the loch. Somehow, she could not bear to look across to the little sheltered cove where Dulmore Lodge lay bathed in pale, wintry sunshine like a remote haven, the grey waters of the loch stretching like a yawning gulf between. It symbolised all her longing, all her heart's yearning, and it was more than she could bear to look upon the unattainable.

Catherine Mailland came to the nursery wing earlier than usual that evening. She had resumed her round of inspection as soon as the night nurse had returned to Edinburgh, but she had found little reason for complaint and had even appeared well pleased. The fact had caused Rhona to hope that her mother-in-law might rescind her decision to find another nurse.

Mrs. Mailland walked once round the day-nursery without speaking, and then she came across to the tea-table where Robin was seated in his high chair, propped firmly with cushions to take the maximum of strain from his back.

"Well, young man! Have you eaten a good tea this afternoon?" she began more affectionately than Rhona had ever heard her speak to the child. "You should have done, since you've been out in the fresh air to-day." She turned to Rhona at last. "How far did you walk, Nurse?"

"Almost to the head of the loch."

"Quite a distance." She looked across at Robin again. "He is pale, of course," she remarked, "but much better, I feel sure. It is a decided relief to see him sitting up there eating as he did before."

"Yes," Rhona whispered, a strangled feeling in her throat which would not permit her to say more.

"I am expecting a nurse to-morrow morning," Mrs. Mailland said abruptly on her way to the door. "If I decide to engage her, she will probably want to see Robin. You go, of course, in a week's time, Grant."

There was to be no reprieve, then? What a fool she had been to expect it—even to wish for it!

Her whole life appeared to be converging to one vital point, and a sudden feeling of helplessness gripped her, leaving her curiously shaken. What else could she suffer? Surely not the complete loss of her child? And then, clear out of the maze and welter of indecision in which she had wandered for weeks past, emerged the one fact that no half-measures with regard to her son would ever suffice. She must have Robin completely or not at all.

Her marriage to Jim Inglis would only be a half-measure. She wondered now that she could ever have thought of it as a solution at all, realising that her grief had blinded her.

Whatever he thought of her, she would go to Neil Murray and seek his help. Once, not so long ago, he had advised her to make a clean breast of everything to the Maillands, but she wanted his assurance first that they could not take Robin from her against her will. In any case, she would tell Neil that she meant to keep her son!

The sleep of utter exhaustion claimed her that night, and she awoke to the pale, winter dawn with the feeling that she had shaken off some heavy burden and was free to walk upright at last.

Her desire to see Neil remained firm and she took her only opportunity. Flora, as she herself had done when she had been junior to Enid Brodie, came on duty at six o'clock, but recently Robin had been sleeping longer in the mornings and she knew that she could leave the nursery for an hour after six without being detected.

It was early, she realised, to pay a call, but her need was paramount. In any case, she was determined to take the chance, knowing that she was prepared to be guided by his decision.

There was only one quick way to reach the other side of the loch, and that was by boat. She must row there and back within the hour.

A rather bewildered Flora received her instructions, and Rhona drew on her coat over her uniform and slipped out of the side door as the clock in the main hall chimed the quarter after six.

As she ran down the drive her mind raced ahead to her meeting with Neil, and she remembered the last occasion when she had sought his advice and had been turned back by Gertrude. Yet, curiously enough, she had no fear of Gretrude Mailland now. She had risen beyond that, and even as she ran, she wondered that she had hesitated so long.

Then her mind turned to the practical side of her adventure. It was quite within the bounds of possibility that the boat-house would be locked.

The padlock was on the chain, but it gave in her fingers, and her heart pounded on in mad relief. The boat slid easily down the keel-run to the water's edge, and she brought out the oars and pushed her small craft onto the glossy surface of the loch. There was not as much as a ripple on the water, and the hills lay reflected in it as in a mirror, the pale sky above them streaked with the rosy aftermath of dawn.

Rhona dipped her oars and the water fell from the blades in glossy beads. Somewhere high above her a bird circled and dipped, rose and circled again.

She pulled steadily and the distance of the loch was halved in little over ten minutes, so swiftly did the tiny skiff glide across the calm water. Dulmore appeared, quiet and white in its sheltered bay, with the strip of golden sand fringing it and the grey rocks shutting it in. It seemed, suddenly, a goal she must reach at all costs, and she bent to the oars with renewed effort.

So tensed was she, so keyed up for the meeting with the man who seemed always to have held her destiny in his hands, that she fastened her boat carelessly and jumped from it onto the jetty without a backward glance, running across the broad strip of lawn, where her shoes made dark footprints on the dew-silvered grass.

It was quarter to seven when she reached the back door. The whole place had the air of being peacefully asleep, and she hesitated, but her need justified it, and finally she raised the heavy knocker and let it fall.

Footsteps sounded on the stone passage-way immediately, and she heaved a quick sigh of relief. The staff, at least, were astir. A maid in a white overall opened the door.

"May I see Mrs. Trigg?"

"She's just come down," the girl said. "I'll go and ask."

Rhona waited. This first uncertain contact had damped her feelings a little, and she began to listen for Jean Trigg's footsteps almost impatiently. They came hurrying along the stone passage a few minutes later.

"Come in, my dear, come in!" Mrs. Trigg invited. "I had no idea who it might be so early in the morning. Is there anything wrong? Not the wee laddie, I hope?"

Rhona stepped into the flagged passage-way leading to the kitchen.

"Robin's all right, Mrs. Trigg," she said, as the housekeeper led the way to the small morning-room at the front of the house where the table was set for breakfast. "It is a disgracefully early hour to call, I know," she rushed on, feeling decidedly nervous now.

"I was up," Jean Trigg assured her. "I always rise at half-past six, summer and winter. I was just going to have my breakfast," she added, crossing to the table. "Will you have some coffee?"

"It's kind of you," Rhona said hastily, "but I mustn't stay. I thought—perhaps Mr. Murray would be up. I—I wanted to see him urgently, Mrs. Trigg. Do you think he would see me—just for a minute or two?"

The old housekeeper was shaking her head.

"You could have seen him," she said, "for he's often up before me, but he has gone to Edinburgh about that massage for his leg. He's no' likely to be back much before Thursday."

"He's gone?"

Rhona echoed the words, feeling that the whole world was collapsing round her.

Jean Trigg was quick to see her distress, and she guessed, also, that it was no trifling matter which had brought her to Dulmore Lodge at this hour of the morning, yet she could not ask for a confidence where none was given.

Rhona stood for a moment, tight-lipped and silent, and in her eyes there appeared suddenly a tired, beaten expression which made her look years older.

"I'm sorry to have given you all this trouble," she found herself murmuring, "but I had no idea Mr. Murray was away. I will have to wait and see him when he comes back from Edinburgh."

"Couldn't you speak to him over the 'phone later in the day?" Jean Trigg suggested helpfully. "He should be at the office in the afternoon. He mentioned some business he had to see to for Miss Mailland, so if you rang up about three o'clock you might catch him."

A ray of hope broke over Rhona's horizon, and she smiled at the woman who had tried to help her.

"Thanks, Mrs. Trigg, I'll do that. I may be lucky and find him in."

"Now sit yourself down and have a cup of coffee before you go back across that cold loch," Jean Trigg commanded. "You've plenty of time."

Rhona submitted to the kindness, though an inward urge seemed to be telling her that she had little time to waste. She glanced at the clock on the mantelpiece as it struck seven. It was not too late, after all, and she had to admit that the hot coffee would be welcome.

When it was brought, the housekeeper poured her out a cup, and sat down to her own meal on the other side of the table.

"Tell me about the wee lad," she encouraged. "I heard from one of the girls that he was out yesterday."

Rhona's eyes glowed.

"Yes, isn't it wonderful! I had him out for over an hour—right to the head of the loch and back. Mrs. Mailland was greatly pleased with his progress."

"Ay! It would have been a levelling blow to Catherine Mailland if anything had happened to her heir!" Jean Trigg laughed. "The old man doesn't come in to their reckoning at all, you know, but a kinder and more courtly old gentleman I've yet to meet. When he comes here I always get my place from him, though I can't say that for Mrs. Mailland and yon daughter of hers. There was some talk—just village chatter, you know—about her and Mr. Neil," she added with a direct look at the girl sitting facing her, "but never a word of truth was there in it."

A sudden glow seemed to encompass Rhona, like a surge of light breaking into a dark room. Was this the truth?

"Mr. Neil knows too much about her," Mrs. Trigg went on. "He's seen too many of her tantrums in the past—one no longer ago than the other evening when she came up here after something she didn't get! Ay, he knows her, and, anyway, Gertrude Mailland's no' his type. He needs a gentle lass," she added tentatively, "one who wouldn't mind that he's likely to walk with a limp for the rest o' his life."

Rhona's eyes grew misty.

"But—Mrs. Trigg—no one would mind that—no one who really cared for him."

"Ay, I've been tellin' him that," Jean Trigg said

huskily, "but a man'll no' always listen to reason when he's got another fool idea in his head."

Rhona sat tensed in her chair, feeling that the older woman's far-seeing hazel eyes were probing deep into her heart.

"I'll have to run now, Mrs. Trigg," she apologised. "It's well after seven."

"I'm sorry you have to go so soon," Mrs. Trigg said. "I'll come down to the jetty with you if you'll wait a second till I get my wee woollen jacket."

"Please don't," Rhona advised. "You haven't finished your breakfast, and I know my way all right. I'm only sorry I have to dash off like this."

"You'll come again, though—one afternoon, maybe, and bring the wee lad to see me when he's a bit better?"

Rhona turned away to hide the sudden trembling of her lips.

"It—would have been lovely to do that, Mrs. Trigg," she managed huskily, "but—I've only got to the end of the month."

Jean Trigg gazed at her, a piece of breakfast roll half-way to her mouth.

"You're leaving?"

"I have been dismissed."

"Dismissed!" The housekeeper snorted. "I wonder if the folks at Kindarroch are in their right mind. Have they anyone to fill your place?"

"There's an applicant coming this afternoon." Suddenly Rhona thought of all this new day was to hold. "I must go—really, Mrs. Trigg. Good-bye— and thank you."

"You're welcome, lass," Jean Trigg said rather flatly. Seemingly a little plan of hers had gone awry somewhere.

Rhona went out by the back door and ran quickly into the shrubbery and down the path leading to the boat-house where she had sheltered on her first visit

135

to Dulmore. Then, as the jetty came into view, she stood aghast.

The boat in which she had rowed over from the Kindarroch side had gone. She could not believe it in that first moment of panic until, shading her eyes against the sun, she saw it floating gently away, carried by the strong currents out beyond the rocks which formed the eastern boundary of Dulmore bay.

What could she do now? Indecision swayed her this way and that, but the dread fact that she was without any means of getting back to Kindarroch in anything like time for breakfast rose uppermost. Her visit to Dulmore would be discovered, or, if she escaped this, there would still be the necessity of explaining about the missing dinghy.

She turned back towards the Lodge with the feeling that her discovery was inevitable—probably had been from the very start of this fruitless adventure.

There was nothing for it but to appeal to Mrs. Trigg for some means of conveyance to the other side of the loch.

When she crossed the lawn and came within sight of the windows, Jean Trigg must have noticed her, for the end window on the low, covered veranda opened and the housekeeper stepped out.

"Come this way, Nurse," she invited. "Have you left something?"

Rhona drew in a quivering breath. "Mrs. Trigg, you're going to think me a terrible nuisance, but—I've let my boat drift away. I mustn't have tied it securely enough when I landed at the jetty."

"That's bad luck," Jean Trigg declared, for she sensed that Rhona's early-morning visit was entirely unofficial. "We'll have to get you across to Kindarroch somehow. I don't suppose you could handle the launch, could you?"

Rhona shook her head, but she asked quickly:

"Would you trust me with Mr. Murray's dinghy, Mrs. Trigg? If I could have it I could row back and perhaps pick up my own boat on the way."

"Of course you can have it!" the housekeeper returned. "Why didn't I think of it right away! Come along and I'll get the key of the boat-house."

Rhona waited until she reappeared with the key and her 'wee woollen jacket,' and followed her portly figure down to the loch. Her eyes sought the Kindarroch boat, and this time it did not seem so very far away. She would make an effort to get it and tow it to safety.

As she rowed out of the bay, the gaunt grey house perched on its rocky pinnacle on the far side of the loch seemed to scowl back at her, detecting her anxiety, and a little shiver, like the premonition of approaching disaster, ran through her.

Yet, so intent was she in retrieving the dinghy, that she steered a course away from Kindarroch which would add a good half-hour to her crossing. It was hopeless now to think of getting back before breakfast, she mused with a dull sort of resignation, but at least she would bring the dinghy back with her.

Not a very expert oarswoman, she found difficulty in securing the drifting boat and taking it in tow. She moved more slowly, too, pulling the two boats, and she was against the current which flowed strongly in the middle of the loch so that it seemed that the Kindarroch shore was receding instead of drawing imperceptibly nearer.

Cutting across the head of the loch, she sought the calmer waters in-shore, and it was not until she was almost parallel with the main gateway of Kindarroch that she was aware of a car being driven slowly along the shore road as if its occupant was particularly interested in her progress. She wondered vaguely who it could be, and when the trees thinned out and she moved in line with the broad drive she saw that it was James Inglis.

The doctor drew his car up at the end of the pathway through the shrubbery, and he was waiting for her on the landing-stage when she shipped the oars and let the dinghy slip in.

"Rhona," he asked sharply, seeing both boats and her flushed and dishevelled condition, "what's the matter? Has anything happened? What took you out on the loch at such an hour?"

She jumped ashore, accepting his proffered hand, but relinquishing it immediately to tie the rope securely to the wooden mooring pole. Her cheeks were flushed and her eyes looked feverish and restless.

"I can't wait to talk now," she said hastily. "I must go, Jim. They'll find out where I've been——"

He barred what might have been sudden flight, taking her firmly by the shoulders.

"And where *have* you been?" he asked.

"I've been to Dulmore," she said rather sharply, because every nerve in her body was tensed with the desire to get back to Kindarroch without further delay. "I—needed advice."

"And you went to Neil for it?" he asked quietly.

"He had gone," she said dully.

James Inglis had experienced faint doubts in the past about his chances of winning Rhona, but now, suddenly, they were a certainty. Something about her—the pinched, hurt look in her eyes, the way she had spoken Neil's name and, above all, the fact that in her troubled state of mind she had sought Neil Murray across the loch before turning to him—told Jim all he needed to know.

"Can't I help?" he asked, "or is it something that only Neil could have done for you?"

She hesitated, glancing over her shoulder at the grey pile of Kindarroch.

"I—wanted advice," she admitted, "but there's

no time to tell you now. Can I see you—somewhere later?"

"Certainly. Anywhere, Rhona."

"This afternoon," she said breathlessly, already moving off up the narrow path. "I will be out with Robin on the Dulmore road."

"I'll be there," he promised. "I started on my calls earlier this morning, thinking to take the afternoon off, anyway."

She thanked him with one swift, grateful look and ran in the direction of the house. At an upstairs window a white hand let the heavy velvet curtains fall back into place, and a woman moved slowly and deliberately from her viewpoint to the door, a look of malicious hatred twisting her thin mouth.

"She was at Dulmore," Gertrude Mailland muttered.

Flora was at the nursery door when Rhona ran breathlessly up the stairs and along the corridor.

"Oh, Miss Grant, Madam's been here," she gasped. "Just a minute or two ago. She heard Robin crying, and I did my best to silence him, but she came along. If only you had managed to get back ten minutes earlier it would have been all right."

Rhona collapsed into a chair, brushing the damp hair from her forehead.

"What did she say?" she asked.

"She wanted to know where you were," Flora began haltingly. "I said—I didn't know."

Rhona smiled wanly.

"It was good of you, Flo, but she'll have to know now, I expect."

"Not if you don't want her to," the girl replied with the air of a conspirator, but Rhona felt suddenly too tired to try to conceal anything further.

It would all come out now, her identity, her deception, her mad journey across the loch at that

139

early hour—everything, and she felt that she did not care.

A bell rang shrilly, and she rose unsteadily to her feet and went out, still in the navy-blue coat in which she had rowed across to Dulmore.

As she passed through the swing doors between the nursery wing and the main hall, she saw Hector Mailland crossing to the morning-room and he turned at sight of her and smiled.

"How's my little lad this morning?"

"He's—well."

Rhona could manage no more for the lump at her throat which threatened to choke her, yet she drew herself up instinctively as she approached the study door. With her hand on the knob, she hesitated. The sound of voices raised angrily came from within, and she stepped back involuntarily as the door opened and her sister-in-law stood frowning at her.

Beyond Gertrude Rhona could see Mrs. Mailland's tall form, but she did not flinch.

"You wanted to see me, Madam?"

Gertrude laughed.

"That's rich! Did you think my mother would condone this morning's little escapade? I rather thought evening shadows were the most fitting background to romance, Grant?" she added vindictively.

"You had better leave us, Gertrude," her mother advised.

Rhona went forward, sitting down on the chair Mrs. Mailland indicated.

"I am not going to ask you what took you out at such a disgraceful hour, Grant," Mrs. Mailland began, "or why you were with Doctor Inglis in his car——"

"Doctor Inglis?" Rhona broke in, realising with a sense of shock that she was being called to account for quite the wrong offence—an offence that seemed ridiculous to her.

"Don't attempt to deny it," Catherine Mailland cautioned. "You were seen."

"By whom, Madam?"

"I consider that rather an impertinent question, Grant, under the circumstances," Mrs. Mailland returned sharply, "but I will answer it. My daughter saw you in the shrubbery with the doctor, and I, myself, recognised his car, and saw him driving away."

Rhona relaxed in her seat. It was all wrong, all mad and stupidly chaotic, but what did it matter? Her eyes were fixed on the little pile of silver coins on the desk before her and she knew their significance. Dismissal at a moment's notice—to-day—now!

"You—want me to go?" she asked, her voice little more than a whisper.

"Surely you are not surprised, Grant, after what has just happened? I warned you before. I am not going to waste words now." Mrs. Mailland picked up the notes and the silver from her desk. "Here are your wages for the full month," she said, "and the references you brought with you. I have been looking up trains," she continued, glancing at a railway guide, "and, leaving time for you to pack, you can catch the five-seventeen from the Junction. The three-ten would be just a little early, I'm afraid. If you have anything at the laundry I will have it sent on," she added practically. "You can leave your address."

Rhona sat deadly still, making no effort to lift either the money or Molly's references.

"I don't want you to go back to your duties in the nursery," Catherine Mailland continued frigidly. "Flora will take them over. I shall engage this woman who is coming to be interviewed to-day. I thought at first that she was rather old, but I believe now that it will be an advantage."

The slight passed Rhona by. She seemed too dazed even to hear her mother-in-law's explanations, and only the fact that Catherine Mailland had decreed that she was not to see Robin again stood out in her tired mind as if it were written there in letters of fire.

"Better go and have your breakfast," Mrs. Mailland advised, and Rhona rose at last and turned blindly to the door. "You've forgotten your money," the older woman reminded her. "You will need it."

She picked up the money and the references and went slowly from the room, looking up listlessly to find Gertrude Mailland standing at the foot of the broad main staircase. There was a cruel smile on her sister-in-law's face, a malignant gleam in her strange, pale eyes.

"So, you're going, Grant?" she said, as Rhona passed her. "And you can't take my nephew with you, can you?"

The words seemed to follow Rhona in a mocking echo as she made her way up the familiar, narrow staircase to the nursery suite for the last time.

For the last time! The agonising truth behind the thought struck her with the force of a physical blow, and she stopped half-way up the stairs, holding onto the oak rail as if for mental as well as physical support.

It could not be! Not the last time she would see Robin! His high-pitched, childish voice floated down the stairs to her through the open door of the day-nursery and the rapping of his spoon on his plate.

Suddenly she was rushing along the white corridor, her hands pressed tightly over her ears to shut out that beloved voice.

When she reached her own room she flung herself down on the iron bedstead under the high window and gazed, wide-eyed and tearless, at the beamed ceiling which slanted down to the wall of the tower.

Walls four feet thick, but not thick enough to exclude the sound of stealthy footsteps on the treacherous stairway beyond, walls that shut her in now, but would so soon divide her from all she held dear. . . . 'You can't take my nephew with you, can you?' . . . Gertrude's hard, vindictive voice and her crafty smile. . . . 'I'd have little compunction in certifying Gertrude insane.' . . . Doctor Jim saying that—and Neil——

Thoughts blazed on in her, giving her no respite. 'You can't take him with you!' That mocking voice echoing always in her ears. 'You can't take him with you!' 'You can't take him——'

She jumped to her feet, her hands shaking as she pulled her suitcase from the bottom of the alcove and began feverishly to pack her clothes, cramming them in any way, gathering her brushes and toilet accessories from the table and pushing them into the flap in the lid, finding shoe-trees and jumpers and hats and packing them in on top as if her very life itself depended upon the speed with which she executed the task.

'You can't take my nephew with you!' It was like a goad now.

She took off her coat and laid it on the bed, going quickly along to the bathroom to sponge her hands and face.

As she bathed her flushed cheeks in the cool water something seemed to slip away from her like an old, discarded cloak. It was fear and nervousness and indecision.

'You can't take him with you!'

Her eyes shone with a resolute gleam, and very quietly she went back along the corridor and paused outside the door of the day-nursery.

"Flora," she called softly.

The girl appeared, pale-faced and afraid.

"I want you to do something for me," Rhona said

steadily. "I'm leaving this afternoon. Would you take my case down to the village for me and leave it at the post office?"

"Certainly, Nurse. I'm sorry you are going——"

"Will you take it now, Flora?"

"Yes, Nurse."

"You can go out by the side door and you will be back before eleven. I'll have Master Robin ready for you to take out in his pram."

The girl slipped into her coat, and Rhona watched her go calmly. It was a calm which seemed to have settled on her very soul, yet her mind was more active than it had ever been before, detached, coolly calculating.

The Maillands were at breakfast and they would remain in the morning-room till round about ten o'clock. There would be no fear of them seeing Flora's depature with the suitcase, for the windows of the morning-room looked out across the lawns to the hills, no fear of them seeing her own departure less than half an hour later.

She hurried back to her room, returning with a small pigskin travelling-bag with a zip fastener across the top and filled it with a change of child's underclothing, a thick woollen coat and a sleeping suit. The remainder of Robin's clothes she left undisturbed in the drawers. Then, very deliberately, she opened the door of the day-nursery where her son was still seated in his chair, and, crossing to the table, took some rusks from a tin, a biscuit or two, and the unopened bottle of pasteurised milk and put them carefully into the bag.

Then, deftly and carefully, she dressed Robin in his outdoor clothes and wrapped him tightly in the blue Otterburn rug which had come with him to Kindarroch from Giffnock.

The descent of the nursery staircase seemed the most perilous she had ever known. Though there was little fear of meeting any of the Maillands, there was the possibility that one of the staff might be encountered either on the stairs or in the hall, and her heart began to beat faster as she rounded the first landing and began the final descent.

The door of Mrs. Norris's parlour was ajar and voices floated out to her—the housekeeper's and the cook's, discussing the menu for the next twenty-four hours. As long as they continued in conversation, she thought breathlessly, they would remain in the little parlour, and she was safe.

She reached the hall and swiftly and noiselessly sped in the direction of the side door, bearing her precious burden carefully in her arms. The door opened easily and she was out in the morning sunshine at last. Behind her the clock in the hall struck ten, the last stroke dying away as she rounded the tower, and approached the one point where she might be seen from the house. It was at the branch of two paths, the one leading through the shrubbery which she must take to reach the main road without using the more exposed drive, the other a narrow pavement running along the edge of the lawn to the terrace steps. Both paths were deserted, but on the steps of the terrace stood a man in nut-brown tweeds throwing a handful of crumbs to the feathered beggars on the lawn.

Hector Mailland! He was looking straight in her direction and her heart turned over in her breast, a cold fear laying icy hands upon her. And then, almost deliberately it seemed, Hector Mailland turned and walked slowly back through the open French windows of the morning-room where the rest of the family were still seated over their coffee.

Rhona could not believe it. She was convinced beyond the shadow of a doubt that her father-in-law had seen her, yet why had he not made any attempt to stop her? It must have been obvious that she had no right to be there with Robin in her arms at this hour and dressed for a journey. Had he gone to tell Mrs. Mailland?

The thought sent her running down the shrubbery path, until she had reached the wooden gate in the boundary wall which led out onto the main road. She leaned against the wall, breathless, her heart still racing at the uncertainty of her escape. Even now the alarm may have been sounded, the nursery searched and the pursuit begun.

Then, suddenly, a strange, calm feeling took possession of her, and she was remembering Hector Mailland as he had knelt beside a captured bird, and freed it, holding it in his hands for his grandson to see; remembering how he had bent over Robin's cot on that dread night of crisis whispering a prayer; remembering how he had come daily to the nursery door after that, quietly, unobtrusively, and thinking that he had often looked at her keenly and smiled.

Did he know? Was it possible that Hector Mailland alone at Kindarroch had guessed her secret?

Steps sounded on the roadway beyond the door, and Rhona paused in the act of opening it, remembering Flora and the fact that she must return this way from the village. The steps were light and, as they approached along the wall, the sound of a popular tune floated across the still morning air. It *was* Flora and she was coming towards the door bent on taking the shorter way home. It was a quarter of a mile farther down the road to the main gates, but Rhona decided swiftly that Flora must walk that extra quarter-mile.

Trembling, she dropped her bag and slipped the rusty iron bolt into place. But for the sound of her own humming, Flora must have heard the rasping of it as it shot home, for the handle was tried almost immediately, and a young exasperated voice exclaimed from the far side:

"Blow it! Who could have locked the door?"

She did not stop to investigate, however, and Rhona drew a deep breath of relief as her footsteps broke to a run and died away down the road.

Robin, becoming impatient at the delay, stirred in her arms. He was no light weight, and already she was beginning to wonder how she was going to carry him the mile and a half to the village. He looked drowsy, too, and she realised that it was time for his morning sleep. If he slept in her arms he would be a dead weight, but she could not help it.

Unbolting the door, she lifted her bag and walked out into the sunshine of the tree-lined road with a determined step.

Robin's eyelids quivered and fell, fluttered open again, and then closed as he snuggled warmly against her. She was glad that he was asleep, though with each step he seemed to become heavier and the bag over her arm became an added burden. Yet she could not rest. Delay was fatal. She had timed everything to a nicety, giving herself just half an hour to reach the village so that she would not be hanging about until the 'bus came in.

Her footsteps began to lag a little as she reached the hill and started the long pull upwards. Could she do it in time? What would happen if she missed the 'bus?

She would not let her mind dwell on such a catastrophe and trudged on, thinking now of the child in her arms whose soft, regular breathing was like the sigh of a little wind strayed among the trees. He was hers again. Hers!

She quickened her steps, and then, suddenly, away behind her, she heard the sound of a car.

Dread seized her as she wondered who it could be. If not the Kindarroch car, it was probably someone in the neighbourhood who would recognise her and wonder, perhaps even stop to question her.

Suddenly she was running, running with futile, stumbling steps while the purring engine came on behind, gaining, ever gaining.

She reached the brow of the hill as the car pulled ahead. It was an old blue saloon, and the single occupant—a woman—looked out as she passed. Then, with a grinding of brakes, the car drew up a little way in front.

Rhona seemed to have lost the power of movement. Every muscle in her body seemed to be throbbing except those of her arms, and they were quite dead. Her hands tightening automatically round her precious bundle, she stood waiting for the blow to fall.

The door on the driver's side swung open, and a woman's head and shoulders appeared.

"Going to the Junction?" the stranger asked.

With an unutterable sense of relief, Rhona realised that she had not been recognised after all. The woman in the car was a complete stranger, and she spoke with an English accent which suggested that she did not belong to these parts at all.

"Jump in," she urged. "That child looks much too heavy for you. Whatever made you attempt to carry him so far?"

"There is no conveyance along this way," Rhona heard herself saying, though the effort to walk round the car seemed suddenly more than she was able to make.

"Here, give me your bag." The woman got out and took the pigskin bag, putting a firm, guiding hand under Rhona's elbow. "You're done in. What train are you going for?"

"I was going for a 'bus—to the village," Rhona explained, sinking thankfully down in the bucket seat and moving Robin's weight from her arms to her knees with a gasp of relief. "It isn't very far," she added, "and the 'bus will be in now, I expect."

New life seemed to be pouring into her veins and her courage, that desperate courage which had taken her from Kindarroch at last, had returned.

"How far are you going?" the stranger asked when she had settled herself at the wheel again.

"Glasgow."

Rhona had uttered the word on the spur of the moment.

"I'm going through to Stirling," the woman at the wheel was saying. "I could take you as far as there if you'd like to come? You could get a train to Glasgow."

Rhona thought swiftly. Was this not a surer way of escape than risking the journey by a 'bus that had many stops between Kindarroch and Perth and could be easily overtaken by a fast private car such as the Maillands had at their disposal?

"Thank you," she accepted, "you are more than kind," and then she thought of the suitcase Flora had carried down to the village for her. "Oh! there's my luggage!" she exclaimed, bitter disappointment in tone and eyes. "I had forgotten. It's at the post-office."

"We can pick it up on the way through," suggested her companion. "There's plenty of room in the back. How much have you got?"

"Just a case."

The stranger pulled up before the post-office.

"You needn't get out," she said kindly. "You'll only disturb the little fellow. I'll get your luggage. What name is it?"

"Molly Grant—Nurse Grant."

Rhona held her breath, not daring to look as her benefactor crossed the cobbled road to the post-office. What if the Maillands had 'phoned? Flora would be back at Kindarroch now and may have been questioned.

The stranger reappeared with the familiar suit-case in her hand.

"Here we are," she announced breezily, tossing it into the back seat. "Feeling a bit easier now, Nurse Grant?"

"Yes," Rhona breathed truthfully, as the car slipped away and Kindarroch and its village were left behind.

Robin slept for the greater part of the journey to Stirling, rocked by the unaccustomed motion of the car, and the woman at the wheel conversed in a low, friendly tone, mostly of her own affairs, seemingly taking no offence at Rhona's obvious reluctance to discuss hers. Rhona learned vaguely that she was a Miss Rhodney-Smith engaged on forestry work and had been in Perthshire for the past month taking a census. It was an interesting job and her whole heart was in it, so that she did not seem to notice that the girl beside her heard but half her tale.

When they reached Stirling Robin was awake, and Miss Rhodney-Smith suggested lunch.

"I've got some milk for the baby," Rhona explained. "Do you think the hotel people would heat it for me?"

"I'll see to it. I know the folks at the Golden Hind quite well," Miss Rhodney-Smith declared. "Here we are! Can you manage all right?"

Rhona got out and stood rather unsteadily on the pavement before the door of the hotel. She was cramped and felt cold, but not hungry. She was too excited to eat, yet she realised that Robin must have something to sustain him.

The hotel was warm, and there was a kindly, wel-coming atmosphere about it which chased the chill feeling from her heart for a moment.

Her companion went off to enquire about lunch and trains for Glasgow, and came back to announce that the lunch was just about to be served and that there was an express due in an hour's time.

"Just fits in nicely, doesn't it?" she observed.

Rhona ate her lunch after she had attended to Robin, and he sat up in a big arm-chair with cushions on both sides of him and smiled at the stranger, while the waitresses lingered in passing, talking to him and bringing him odd little trinkets to play with—a bell, a chromium crumb-tray, the padded beater from a little silver gong.

It did not seem that the journey had harmed him. That had been Rhona's one big worry, the risk she had almost hesitated to take.

Miss Rhodney-Smith drove her to the station and there they parted. For her kindness alone, and the fact that she had shown no inclination to probe into her private affairs, Rhona realised that she would never forget her.

Robin enjoyed the journey to Glasgow. He sat up on her knee and gazed out of the window, bewildered but enchanted by the panorama of flashing fields and cows and sheep, there one minute, gone the next.

She took a taxi from Buchanan Street to Giffnock, and when it turned into the familiar road and ran smoothly along beside the kerb to come to rest outside the bungalow, she experienced a sudden desire to cry.

Yet tears were silly, weakening things, and she had no time for them now. She paid the driver, and he opened the gate for her and carried her suitcase up the path.

Opening the door with her latchkey, she took Robin inside. How small and cramped the little hall seemed after the cold spaciousness of Kindarroch, and yet how utterly dear it was!

She laid the child down on the settee in the little drawing-room as he was, hastily opening windows to let in the fresh air.

"We've come home, Robin," she whispered. "Nanny has brought you home!"

CHAPTER SEVEN

NEIL MURRAY drove his car in between the open gates of Dulmore Lodge with a sense of impatience which had gripped him all day and sent him tearing back from Edinburgh with a doctor's final verdict ringing in his ears. It was the verdict he had expected; not a spectacular verdict, not the miracle of a complete cure, but better, in some ways, than he felt he had any right to expect when he reviewed the nature of his accident and the complete wreck he had been less than a year ago. He would walk at last, even without the aid of a stick, though there would always be a limp. Thank heaven, he mused, he had their assurance that the pain would go eventually, and he would not be an intolerable burden to those around him.

Those around him? He smiled wryly at the thought. Mrs. Trigg and his father. Who else?

The thought of Rhona Mailland flashed through his mind like a meteor, leaving a trail of light behind, but he turned from it half savagely. What right had he . . . ?

Jean Trigg ran out of the door at the first sound of the car.

"I got your 'phone message," she said as Neil hobbled across to her. "Could you no' keep away?"

"I couldn't!" he returned. "There wasn't much use my staying in Edinburgh once I had heard my fate."

They were in the house now, and Jean was almost afraid to ask him what the doctors had said.

"Is it absolutely final this time, Mr. Neil?" she asked.

"Absolutely." He led the way into the study where a great log fire burned cheerfully on the open hearth. "Their first verdict stands, I'm afraid. There will always be—the limp."

"But it's nothing, really," she said quickly. "It's a miracle that you're to do without your sticks in time." Suddenly she was thinking of little Nurse Grant and their conversation in the morning-room only a few hours before. "You shouldn't be sensitive about it, Mr. Neil," she declared stoutly. "Nurse Grant was just saying how foolish that was."

"Where did you see her?" he asked, still gazing out through the long panel of the window facing the drive.

"She came early," Mrs. Trigg replied. "She wanted to see you."

He turned at that, his face concerned.

"Was it urgent? Did she say what she wanted?"

"She didn't say. I think she was most disappointed to find you had gone, and it must have been pretty urgent to bring the lass across the loch at seven o'clock in the morning."

"She came here—at that hour?" Jean Trigg saw his hands clench on his sticks. "It must have been urgent, Mrs. Trigg. Didn't she leave any sort of message for me at all?"

"None. I advised her to 'phone the Edinburgh office, but I didn't know then that you were coming home," the housekeeper explained. "I 'phoned Kindarroch twice after I got your message to try to get in touch with her, but each time the number was engaged and I couldn't get through."

"I must see her at once." He moved towards the door. "She may need my help. Something seems to have gone wrong."

"Won't you have a bite to eat first?" Mrs. Trigg asked, her first thought of his welfare. "I have it all ready."

"I had a spot of lunch before I left Edinburgh," he said, drawing on his gloves. "Will it keep, Mrs. Trigg. I've a feeling this is urgent."

When the car had disappeared round the bend in the drive, she remembered that she had not told him the other half of this morning's adventure and that his dinghy was pulled up somewhere on the Kindarroch shore, but she dismissed it as irrelevant and went quickly into his bedroom to unpack his bag.

Neil would not have considered it irrelevant, however, and the information was conveyed to him even before he reached Kindarroch.

He drove faster than usual, completing the journey round the shore road in record time, and as he neared the Kindarroch drive another car swung in between the gates, and he recognised the driver immediately.

James Inglis drew up as he came abreast, his face grave, his eyes curiously strained.

"What's the matter, Jim?" Neil asked quickly. "Have you been sent for? Is there anything wrong?"

"I'm not quite sure." James Inglis was looking at him queerly, almost guardedly, Neil thought. "I had a 'phone call just after lunch," he went on. "Mrs. Mailland sounded decidedly agitated, and she wouldn't say anything over the 'phone, but she told me to come over immediately. That was impossible, as it happened, and I'm on my way up now for the first time."

"Do you think it is something in connection with Rhona?"

The doctor nodded.

"I'm afraid so. By the way," he asked, "when did you get back?"

"Half an hour ago. I came over right away. Rhona evidently tried to see me this morning."

James Inglis looked across the loch.

"That's probably the reason for the rumpus,

though, at the moment, I can't quite connect myself with Mrs. Mailland's anger."

"What the devil do you mean?" Neil asked shortly.

"Well, it's like this, as far as I can see," Inglis explained. "Rhona was terribly worried over something this morning, and rowed across to see you about it—to ask your advice, I suppose." He steadied his voice and continued: "Unfortunately her boat drifted away while she was talking to Mrs. Trigg, and she wasted a good deal of precious time getting it back. I happened to meet her when she landed here and, frankly, Neil, she was in a bit of a state."

"Was there nothing you could have done?" Neil asked sharply.

"I offered my help—naturally—but she was late and dead scared of being found out at that early hour. That's my point," the doctor added. "Has that old tyrant up at Kindarroch found out? If so, we're in for a scene."

Neil pressed his starter and the engine purred into life. His mouth was set and grim.

"I'm not beating about the bush any longer over this business," he said. "I'm going on up there. Are you coming, Jim? Rhona may need us."

James Inglis hesitated.

"There's something else——"

"Yes?"

"When I asked Rhona if I could help, she said she needed advice and told me to meet her when she was out with the boy this afternoon." His eyes met those of the other man squarely. "She didn't turn up," he added briefly.

"Heavens! Do you think——?"

"I think," James Inglis said deliberately, his voice carrying above the sound of Neil's engine, "that when we get to Kindarroch we will find that Rhona has gone."

155

"Somehow, Jim, I'm not surprised. Do you blame her?" Neil said after a minute's reflection.

"Not one bit. I only hope no harm comes to the boy."

Neil sat silently for a moment.

"What must she be thinking of us?" he said at last, "failing her like this!"

"My one regret is that I did not go up to the house with her," the doctor confessed.

"We must go now," Neil declared, letting in his clutch.

The two cars raced swiftly up the drive and came to a standstill at the main doorway. Neil rang the bell, and Mrs. Norris answered the summons herself.

The housekeeper's eyes were grave and concerned-looking, but she ushered them into the hall without a word.

"Mrs. Mailland is waiting to see you, Doctor Inglis," she said briefly. "Will you come this way?"

"You may as well come along, Neil," Inglis said, and Neil followed them across the hall.

"Doctor Inglis, Madam, and Mr. Neil Murray from Dulmore."

Neil knew that the announcement of his name had been a complete surprise to all the occupants of the study, especially to Gertrude. She half rose in her chair, and a dull colour stained her sallow cheeks as their eyes met across the room.

"Come in." Mrs. Mailland was seated at her desk, her back to the light. "I'm glad you've come, Neil. I would have sent for you immediately, but I understood you were in Edinburgh."

"I was—until this morning."

"Well, I am glad you are here now. I may need your advice." Catherine Mailland's eyes left his face and travelled quickly to the doctor. "I sent for you, Doctor Inglis, because I feel you may be able to shed some light on this wretched business of my grandson's disappearance," she added curtly.

James Inglis's level glance met Neil's for an instant.

"I'm afraid I am going to be quite unable to help you," he said slowly and very deliberately.

"Do you mean you *refuse* to help?"

Gertrude's cold, metallic tones cut across the silence, but the doctor ignored her. He continued to look at Mrs. Mailland, waiting for her to speak.

"You are not going to deny that you were one of the last people to speak to Nurse Grant?" Catherine Mailland challenged. "You can't deny that she was with you for some considerable time this morning— plotting this outrage, I should not wonder, in your car. Why else should she rise at such an hour in order to meet you?"

"You're making a mistake, Mrs. Mailland." It was Neil who spoke, limping forward to confront the older woman, his young face harsh in the full glare of the light from the long windows behind her. "Nurse —Grant came to Dulmore to see me."

"You——? Neil, what are you talking about?"

"I promised her the benefit of my advice if ever she should need it," he said slowly, "and I am only sorry that I failed her this morning by being out of reach."

"Advice? What are you saying?" For the first time in his life Neil Murray saw a wave of intense feeling sweep over Catherine Mailland's face. "Do you realise that Nurse Grant has kidnapped my grandson? Are you talking about offering advice to a person who has committed—a felony?"

"My advice would not have altered the situation," Neil replied sternly, though, curiously enough, he felt suddenly sorry for the woman who faced him.

"I can't understand you!" Even her voice was shaken. It hardened, however, as she continued:

"You may take her part—though why, I am at a complete loss to understand—but that girl has committed a crime and she will be made to answer for it to the law." She bent forward, her hand going out to the telephone. "It's kidnapping, Neil, and I'm going to 'phone for the police."

"I wouldn't do that, if I were you!" The steely tone of Neil's voice arrested her as effectively as if he had struck her hand from the instrument. "Rhona has only taken her own."

"Rhona——?"

It was Gertrude who uttered the name in one quick, bewildered gasp.

"Alan's wife!" Catherine Mailland whispered, aghast.

Neil continued to look at the older woman.

"Yes," he said. "Nurse Grant, as you called her, has taken her son."

There was a hush in the room that could almost be felt, and Neil heard Gertrude's heavy breathing behind him before Mrs. Mailland spoke.

"This is preposterous!" she cried, though even before she ended there was a note of doubt in her voice. "I can't believe such a thing could have happened here—under my own roof—and that I should not suspect. It's—quite ridiculous," she repeated, as if to convince herself.

"I'm not so sure, Mother," Gertrude reflected slowly, her pale eyes on Neil with a sudden bitter venom in their depths, for Gertrude Mailland, finding herself the woman scorned, could hate as vigorously as she had loved. "Obviously you sent a strange ambassador to Glasgow when you decided to take Alan's child."

Catherine Mailland started like a sleeper awakened from a nightmare dream.

"Yes, of course," she said, confronting Neil. "You went to see her in the first place!" She broke off, realisation dawning in her aloof eyes, and behind that realisation a bitter disappointment. "Neil, you must have known this all along—known how we were being deceived—exploited by this girl——"

"Deceived, perhaps," Neil broke in, "but never exploited. Rhona would never have sought to gain anything for herself out of this wretched bargain. She wasn't like that. She gave you good and faithful service for the privilege of being near her son."

"I paid her well," Mrs. Mailland declared. "She only did her duty."

"A little more than that," Neil said firmly. "Jim Inglis will tell you that, but for her devotion, your grandson would never have survived his accident."

"And but for her carelessness it would never have occurred!"

Gertrude's cold, unemotional tones cut across the silence, and both men turned sharply in her direction. Neil found himself wondering how she had the audacity to discuss the accident which was so surely her crime, and the doctor said scathingly:

"I think you'll agree that we should not go into the subject at the moment."

"Yes, there's nothing to be gained by rushing off at a tangent," Mrs. Mailland said almost wearily. "We are discussing the fact that my grandson has been—taken away without my authority, and I want to know what Neil considers the quickest and surest way of getting him back. I should have thought—the police——"

"You wouldn't have even the beginning of a case in law," Neil assured her bluntly. "The child's mother has removed him from your house because she was turned out of it, and that's all there is to it."

"But she agreed—she gave him to us." Mrs. Mailland's voice hardened. "There must be some sort of protection for us."

"Rhona did not sign anything," Neil said briefly.

"You did not adopt the boy in any legal sense. It was a mutual agreement, and Rhona gave way to it because she expected that her child would have a better chance in life here."

"I suppose you gave her the benefit of your advice about refusing to sign anything?" Gertrude flung out coldly.

Neil's mind went back to that afternoon in the bungalow at Giffnock, and he smiled faintly.

"I did," he admitted. "I thought she stood rather badly in need of advice."

"Neil," Catherine Mailland said, "I can't understand you! You were always such a good, reliable boy——"

"I'm sorry," he returned gravely, "if you think that I have done you a disservice, Mrs. Mailland, but I can't pretend to be in anything but the fullest sympathy with your daughter-in-law."

Catherine Mailland flushed at the name.

"Do you know, then, why she has done this?" she demanded, still speaking mainly to Neil. She seemed to have forgotten the doctor entirely.

"I think—because she was unhappy here, and she had come to realise that a child as young as Robin need's a mother's care," he replied slowly, "even more than a vast heritage."

"There was nothing he could not have had at Kindarroch," Mrs. Mailland said almost wistfully. "Nothing!"

"Except mother-love."

Neil was surprised at the intensity of his own words even as he uttered them, but he found to his amazement that the effect they had on the woman before him was not what he had expected. Anger died in Catherine Mailland's eyes, and they were no longer aloof. Something had sprung to life in them, warming them a little.

"So you think we offered the boy a—sort of bleak heritage?" she asked awkwardly.

"It would have been different," he said, "if you had given his mother a chance, too. As it was, you judged her most harshly before you had even met her."

She drew herself up at that, all her pride in arms.

"How dare you say such a thing, Neil! Do you know what you are inferring?" she demanded. "That I have been unjust—overbearing—disloyal to Alan, even!"

He continued to gaze at her steadily.

"You have been—just that," he said slowly.

She gave a queer, strangled sort of gasp, and sat down in her chair, looking suddenly years older as her erect shoulders hunched forward in a beaten attitude which was rather pitiful to see.

"Neil," she said in a strained whisper, "I should order you out of the house for that."

"I am ready to go," he said unemotionally.

"No—wait!" She sat up, staring unseeingly beyond him. "There may be something you can do for me."

"I wonder that you feel like trusting Neil again!"

Gertrude rose from her chair, but at sight of her mother's tense, set face and the angry gleam in her eyes she halted half-way to the desk.

"I think you should leave us, Gertrude," Mrs. Mailland said sternly. "When I need your advice in future I shall ask you for it."

Gertrude turned away with an ugly, baffled expression in her eyes and her mouth twisting in a bitter sneer.

"Very well. If you prefer the counsel of strangers ——!"

She shrugged significantly, and went from the room.

"I don't think we can do very much," Neil said

1440 161

as soon as she had gone. "We certainly can't force Rhona to return here against her will."

"I wasn't thinking of trying to force her," Catherine Mailland replied, "but—I find that I want my grandson. I want him to inherit Kindarroch because it is his by right."

Long afterwards, Neil realised that it was the seemingly unimportant fact that Catherine Mailland had mentioned her desire for Robin before her desire for an heir for Kindarroch that made him promise:

"If I can do anything for you, Mrs. Mailland, I will."

She thanked him rather heavily and rose to her feet, and though she appeared shorn of some of the dignity which had been her most distinguishing feature, he thought that she looked more human for it.

"Will you come to see me to-morrow?" she asked. "Seemingly, we can do nothing to-day."

Neil assured her that he would, and followed Jim Inglis from the room. When they were out in the sunshine at last, he stood for a moment as if not quite sure what to do next.

"Come back with me," Jim suggested. "We can talk this out at my place—if you want to discuss it?"

"It would be a relief," Neil admitted. "I'll follow you."

James Inglis's house stood on the main road, a big, square sandstone building with many windows and an arched doorway over which hung a curiously carved lantern, bearing his name.

"Come into my den," he invited when he had let himself in with a latchkey. "We can have some tea there, and I hope I won't be disturbed before evening surgery."

Neil settled himself in one of the deep leather arm-chairs in the typically mannish room and felt for his pipe. Jim Inglis rang for tea, and they sat smoking in silence until it was brought in on a big tray and set out on the gate-legged table pulled up to the fire.

"I wonder where she is at this moment?"

It was the doctor who broke the silence.

"I'd give anything in this world to know," Neil said, his love manifest in words and expression alike. "I feel that we have failed Rhona miserably."

James Inglis stirred restlessly.

"Yes, we've put up a pretty poor show—both of us."

"Would she go to Glasgow, do you think?" Neil asked.

The doctor shook his head.

"I hardly think so. It would be too obvious if she thought that she might be pursued."

Neil flinched at the word.

"That's it," he said bitterly. "I feel that I, of all people, have the least right to follow her."

His companion sat up in his chair, his eyes narrowed a little.

"In my opinion," he said, "you have the greatest right—the only right, in fact."

Neil looked back at him quite steadily.

"Why do you think that?"

"At the risk of taking all the wind clean out of your sails," Jim told him almost defiantly, "because I know you care for Rhona, and—I believe she is in love with you."

His words fell into a silence which was tense and a little grim.

"That," Neil said at length, "is the very last possibility."

"How do you know?"

"Because," Neil returned quietly, "I was right at the bottom of all this business and——"

"Yes——?"

"Well, dash it all, you don't expect a woman to tie herself to a man who's going to limp around on two sticks all his life—even if she could bring herself to forgive that first error of judgment."

"I'm glad you called it that," James Inglis remarked. "As for the sticks, didn't you tell me they were merely a temporary embarrassment?"

"Yes," Neil returned, "but I'll never be quite the partner a woman would dream of——"

"You're looking at superficialities now," the doctor told him in some exasperation, "and, as I see it, it's rather an insult to Rhona. If she loves you—and I believe she does—her eyes have already gone deeper—much deeper—than the surface."

"So, you think I should go and find her?" Neil asked.

"I think so."

The doctor watched a new light breaking in the younger man's eyes and Neil seemed to be standing more erect when he rose at last.

"She may resent it," he reflected aloud as they stood at the door together, "but we'll have to take our chance of that."

Catherine Mailland was seated in a deep velvet arm-chair before the fire in the small drawing-room when Neil was shown in at eleven o'clock the following morning.

He had spent a sleepless night, his anxiety for Rhona mounting with each passing hour, and he had cursed himself a thousand times for not going after her immediately he had learned of her flight or even after that illuminating conversation in Jim Inglis's study.

Now, however, the best part of another day lay before him and he hoped that he would have made some form of contact with her before nightfall. He chafed at the delay caused by this promised visit to

Kindarroch and meant to cut the interview short at the earliest possible opportunity.

"Come in, Neil," Mrs. Mailland invited, indicating a chair near her own. "I thought you would have come earlier. I have been waiting for you."

Her tone surprised Neil as he sat down facing her. Gone was the note of anger tinged with bitter disappointment which had been uppermost yesterday and in its place was something like appeal. Glancing at her in the revealing morning light, he saw the lines of fatigue and mental strain clearly marked about eyes and mouth, though there was still a faint hint of that old, aloof pride about her which she would never lose, no matter what happened.

"Hector will be here in a moment," she said, and the remark surprised Neil even more than the evidence that something had touched Catherine Mailland's heart at last. Was it possible that Hector Mailland was to be consulted now?

He came in, unobtrusive as ever, in his brown tweeds.

"Ah, Neil, here you are my boy!" he greeted warmly. "I hope you are going to be able to help us."

"It depends," Neil found himself saying, "in what way you want my help."

There was a short, rather strained silence and then Mrs. Mailland spoke.

"I will be frank with you," she said. "We both feel that there has been some dreadful mistake about —about Alan's wife right from the beginning."

It had been a hard confession to make, Neil realised, but he admired Catherine Mailland for making it immediately instead of grudgingly when matters were too late to mend.

"Hector was not—very surprised to hear your news about Nurse Grant," Mrs. Mailland went on more steadily. "He had partly guessed her real identity during the period of Robin's recovery from that dreadful accident which, by the way, I feel still remains unexplained."

Neil thought bitterly that he could have given her an explanation that would have staggered her, but what was the use? Certainly he believed that it had been Gertrude's mad act which had been the chief cause of Rhona's departure, but he also knew that Rhona would never have been really happy living at Kindarroch under an assumed name.

"I will help you if I can," he found himself promising, and went on to stipulate: "I will be no party, however, in any scheme to separate Rhona and her child a second time."

The colour rose in Catherine Mailland's cheeks and her husband spoke for both of them.

"We have no wish to separate them, Neil. We want them back here—together."

Neil, thinking of Gertrude, said rather brusquely:

"I'm not at all sure that she would return now, even on those terms."

Catherine Mailland rose, walking quickly to the window and back again.

"We're trying to make some sort of amends, Neil," she observed somewhat accusingly.

"I know," he said, "and it's very hard to tell you that it might be impossible now."

"We must make some effort to do so," Hector Mailland said quietly. "You will not stand in our way, Neil, surely?"

Neil shook his head.

"Have you any idea where she may be found?" Mrs. Mailland asked. "Don't you think she would return to Glasgow?"

"I don't suppose so—if she was anxious not to be followed."

"Did she give up her home?"

"No—I don't think she did."

"Then—perhaps if we made enquiries there—?"

"It's doubtful if we'd meet with success."

Something reluctant seemed to be stirring within Neil, something that urged him instinctively to keep Mrs. Mailland from the bungalow at Giffnock until he had made his own attempt to find Rhona.

"We must try, though. It means a great deal to us," she said. "We became very attached to the child while he was with us."

"Even this one day without him has seemed a terrible gulf in time," Hector Mailland put in. "To older people, Neil, a young child coming among them is like a renewal of their own youth—their happier years."

The wistful appeal struck the last doubt from Neil Murray's mind. He must go all out to help them—to make Rhona realise this change of heart.

"If you can trust me," he said slowly, conscious that he was speaking more to the elderly man in brown tweeds than to the tall, handsome woman standing erect and expectant before him, "I will try to find Rhona for you, but I must ask you to let me do it in my own way—to go alone."

Mrs. Mailland's brows met in a frown.

"I can't see why you must ask this," she said. "I am quite able to put my proposition to—my daughter-in-law myself."

"Give him his way," her husband advised. "He has probably some good reason for asking."

"I have," Neil returned. "Forgive me for not sharing it with you for the moment, but I feel it would be best if I spoke to Rhona first."

"I can't see the point," Mrs. Mailland remarked, but she raised no further objection to Neil's plan, only adding: "Will you go to Glasgow first?"

"I think so. I may find some sort of contact there. Even an indirect one would be better than none." Neil glanced at his watch. "I can catch the three-ten express from the Junction."

"Will you stay to lunch?" Catherine Mailland asked. "I can have it put forward half an hour."

"No—thanks all the same." Neil felt that he had to get away, to be alone for an hour to think. "Mrs. Trigg will be expecting me, and I'd better have a bag packed in case I decide to stay in Glasgow."

"We shouldn't really be giving you all this trouble," Hector Mailland said as he walked to the door with his visitor. "You're not fit yet, but it means a lot to us and—maybe she'd listen to you."

Strangely enough, mused Neil as he drove away, he had not felt as fit for months, and yet he still walked with the aid of his stick.

Mrs. Trigg did not seem unduly astonished when he asked her to pack a bag and told her his mission.

"I'm no' greatly surprised," was her blunt way of putting it. "The Maillands were aye ready to get others to pu' their chestnuts out o' the fire for them. All I'm saying to ye, Mister Neil, is watch ye don't get yoursel' sair burned in the process."

To this seemingly obscure remark Neil vouchsafed no reply; he had other and more important things to think of at the moment, he told himself.

"Don't forget to take care o' yoursel'." Jean admonished as she stood at the door watching the chauffeur start up the car that was taking him as far as the Junction. "You're no' really fit to be going jauntin' off to strange hotels, you know!"

Neil sat back in his seat and gave himself up to thoughts of Rhona on the way to the station. He sat in the car talking to the chauffeur until the train came whistling round a bend far up the line and then he got out and walked slowly onto the platform.

There was only one other passenger waiting for the three-ten express and she came towards him swiftly as the train steamed in.

"I've changed my mind, Neil," Catherine Mailland informed him. "I'm coming with you."

CHAPTER EIGHT

RHONA sat for some time in the bungalow wondering what she should do next, and then she was startled by a loud knock on the front door.

She jumped to her feet, her heart pounding madly as her mind leapt wildly to thoughts of the police, but she picked Robin up in her arms and walked resolutely towards the door.

Opening it, she almost wept with relief at sight of her visitor. The woman on the tiled step came in without being asked.

"I saw the taxi coming into the Avenue and I could not believe my eyes when it pulled up at your door," Mrs. Rush from the bungalow at the corner explained. "I hope you don't think I'm butting in, but I wondered if you were thinking of staying here to-night, my dear."

Rhona smiled faintly.

"I *had* thought of it, Mrs. Rush.

Her neighbour tried to hide her surprise. She was a woman who never indulged in gossip and did not resent the fact that Rhona did not offer further confidence.

"You must come to me," she suggested, fondling one of Robin's chubby hands.

"It's—so kind of you, Mrs. Rush." Rhona swallowed hard. "But I can't impose on you like that——"

Her neighbour took Robin out of her arms.

"Listen to her!" she addressed him in her simple, homely way. "And you just fair ready for a glass of warm milk and a nice long sleep!"

The remark sealed Rhona's wavering decision. For Robin's sake she must accept the Rush's hospitality and hope to repay them somehow.

"We'll put on fires here after tea," her neighbour suggested, as they went out into the hall and Rhona lifted her bag from the wooden settle behind the door. "That is, if you are going to stay."

"I don't know—I'm not quite sure. . . ."

Joe Rush, who was working on night-shift, brought Robin's old cot from the bungalow and the mattress from one of the girls' small beds was used as a makeshift for the night. The whole family seemed to be putting themselves out to make her welcome and she felt at home among them.

The evening went in more quickly than she had imagined and when Mr. Rush went out at nine o'clock Rhona found herself seated over the fire with his wife confiding part of her story to the older woman with an immeasurable sense of relief.

"You did right to take him with you," Mrs. Rush said, "and to-morrow we must see what's to be done about it. If you were asking my advice I'd just tell you to bide where you are in your own home and defy the lot o' them. They can't take the bairn from you if you've signed nothing. But we'll see in the morning what's to be done."

When the morning came, however, Rhona was less sure about remaining at Giffnock than ever, though, so far, she had not been able to think of a single alternative. Mrs. Rush helped to solve her problem of the moment.

"Would you not stay with us for a wee while?" she suggested. "With Mabel away at her hospital training, we've the extra bedroom, and you're welcome to it till you make up your mind what you want to do."

Rhona thought over the proposition all morning and after their mid-day dinner she said:

"I'll stay, Mrs. Rush, for a day or two—even, maybe, a week or two—if you'll have me as a paying guest."

The older woman looked as if she was about to

refuse the last stipulation, and then she said simply:

"I'll have you any way you like to come!"

Rhona walked in the park that afternoon, pushing the old pram, and a thousand memories came crowding back to her; memories of happiness and that one desperate memory of overwhelming sorrow that she would never, never be able to forget.

As she walked back to the Avenue it seemed that she was re-living the hours of that dreadful day when she had parted with Robin and come to the park only to rush madly back to the bungalow too late.

Feverishly her thoughts drove her onwards and she quickened her pace, drawing up only when she realised that a taxi was standing at the gate of her home this time, too. She drew back involuntarily, turning the pram into Farnham Drive, and waited.

A man came slowly from the taxi, and suddenly every pulse in her body was quivering at sight of the tall figure leaning slightly over two walking-sticks.

"Neil!"

The name escaped her parted lips and then seemed to be frozen there as Mrs. Mailland followed Neil out onto the pavement.

Rhona's fingers tightened convulsively around the handle of the pram. She could not move, and she felt that all the world was crashing round her. Neil! Neil had brought Mrs. Mailland to Giffnock to find her—Neil, who was the only one who could have guessed the confused state of her mind and known that she would come home first of all until she was able to think more clearly—Neil had led the pursuit. . . .

Her whole body was convulsed by a great shivering sob and something seemed to be breaking up in her breast, something fragile and beautiful that he had set in her heart, and in its place was left a terrible emptiness.

She watched as the visitors to the bungalow knocked at the door and waited, glad with a sort of weary elation that she had not lit fires in any of the rooms and so given her presence away. Mrs. Mailland came down the path and went next door, presumably make to enquiries, and Rhona waited breathlessly. There was no reply, however, and her mother-in-law stood at the gate contemplating the waiting taxi. Neil joined her after a few minutes, and Rhona drew back, though they were both looking the other way.

She knew that she ought to be angry, but she felt nothing, only an empty, gnawing ache at her heart that was more than disappointment, 'Neil! Neil!' something seemed to be protesting within her in a dying voice, 'how could you do this? How could you do this to me!'

Anger would come, she thought numbly; it was the natural sequence to such a betrayal, but there was only the broken feeling within her even after the sense of physical paralysis had lifted and she was able to walk further along Farnham Drive until she was sure that the taxi had pulled away from her door and was out of sight.

It meant that she could not stay here, that she would have to leave the Rushs'—leave Glasgow—for there was nothing to assure her that Mrs. Mailland—and Neil—would not return.

The sudden desire for Margaret Rush's kindly advice made her turn and walk swiftly back to her neighbour's bungalow at the corner where she was welcomed at the open door by a kindly smile that seemed to tear her heart apart.

"Did you see them?" Mrs. Rush asked. "Two people at your gate in a taxi?"

Rhona wheeled the pram into the narrow hall, closing the door firmly behind her as if to shut out the world.

"Yes," she said huskily, "it was my mother-in-law and—and her solicitor."

"You know," said Mrs. Rush quietly as the unfastened Robin's coat, "I had an idea it was someone like that. That's why I didn't come out to meet you. I didn't want them to stop me and ask questions."

"They—may come back." Rhona still stood as if she must depart then and there in order to be safe. "I can't stay here, Mrs. Rush—I mustn't. If they come back they will take Robin from me. There must be some legal way when—when——"

She broke off, unable to force herself to utter Neil Murray's name. He, who had befriended her and in whom she had risked so much to confide, had turned his allegiance to the Maillands again!

"I must get away," she repeated as they sat down to their tea. "Do you know anywhere, Mrs. Rush—a quiet, country place where I could take Robin for a little while?"

Her neighbour considered.

"I've a sister at Inellen," she said at last. "She might be able to take you." She rose to clear the table, adding practically: "I'll go down with you and see what she says, anyway."

Rhona went to bed early that night, though she knew she would not sleep. A thousand times she wondered if she was doing right, and, if she dozed fitfully, it was to summon up the vision of Alan, her dead husband, who looked sadly at her with the hint of accusation in his eyes. He had wanted Robin to have his heritage, but he could not have known what his people would do to her—what Gertrude was like. . . .

She lay thus until Robin awoke, whimpering, in the night, and instantly she was out of bed and bending over the cot, whispering soothing words of reassurance, thinking that the strange surroundings had made him nervous.

Though her voice pacified him, however, they did not still his restless tossing and more than once before the morning he was awake again. When dawn broke, Rhona found him flushed and feverish, and her worst fears were realised. The journey from Kindarroch had been too much for him in his weakened state. It had been too soon after his accident.

Almost impatiently she waited for the sound of Mrs. Rush's footsteps coming along the corridor to prepare her husband's meal when he came in from the factory at seven o'clock. The older woman seemed to have lain longer this morning—or was it her own impatience and anxiety that made the time seem so long before the heavy footfall came past her door.

Instantly she opened it, standing there, a slim, anxious figure in her green dressing-gown with her hair ruffled and her eyes dark-circled and pleading as she asked:

"Have you a minute, Mrs. Rush, to look at Robin?"

Her neighbour came into the room immediately and crossed to the cot.

"He's been restless all night and—I thought he looked feverish?"

"His eyes are a wee heavy and his brow's hot," Margaret Rush agreed, "but it may be nothing but teeth, the old bugbear!"

"There was the journey," Rhona pointed out. "Oh, Mrs. Rush, if anything happens to him now I will never forgive myself! I——"

The older woman put a kindly arm round her shoulder.

"Now, don't go meeting trouble half-way, my dear," she advised. "I don't think it's very much, but we won't go to Inellen to-day, just in case it *was* the journey that upset him, and if you still feel doubtful, why don't you take him along to old Doctor Jordan? Explain about the accident and see what he says. He'll give you good advice, and he brought Robin into the world, didn't he?"

Rhona nodded, relieved by her friend's assurance and realising that her suggestion was a most practical one.

The visit to her old medical practitioner reassured her completely. Margaret Rush had been right about 'the old bugbear' of cutting teeth, and the doctor even advocated the change of air when Rhona told him of the proposed visit to Inellen.

"Take him," he advised, "by all means, but go to the doctor there and explain his case and he will keep an eye on him. I think you'd better do that, Mrs. Mailland."

Rhona went back to the Rushs' bungalow in a happier state of mind as far as Robin was concerned, though she looked quickly down the length of the Avenue before she walked briskly in through the gateway and wheeled the pram quickly round to the back door.

"Mrs. Rush," she called breathlessly, "he's all right! The doctor even said he could travel. Do you think—would you go with me to-morrow to your sister's?"

"I think we'd better go this afternoon," Margaret Rush said, and Rhona noticed for the first time that her lips were firmly compressed, her habitually calm expression disturbed.

"Has—anything happened?"

"That gentleman who was at your place yesterday—your mother-in-law's solicitor—was back this morning. If he had come along Farnham you would have met him, but he came up from the main road," Margaret Rush explained.

Rhona went deadly white and her heart began to race madly at the thought of Neil. He had come again, alone this time, but she could not doubt that he had come as Mrs. Mailland's messenger. He was seeking her still—to destroy this new-found happiness, for she was happy in possession of her son, though not entirely at peace. She thought that peace would never come to her again.

"We'll go," she said, and there was a note of unconscious defiance in her tone. "We'll go at once, because—because he will come back," she added in a whisper.

It seemed to Rhona that she had gone through the past two days in a dream, leaving the more practical side of all the arrangements to Margaret Rush and her sister.

Mrs. Cameron had agreed to make room for her as soon as she had heard part of her story, and Rhona was installed in a bedroom overlooking the sea and given a small sitting-room underneath for her private use. Andrew Cameron, a retired postman, seemed to have taken root in the easy-chair beside the kitchen range, so that his wife declared she was glad to have someone to use the sitting-room, if only to keep it fired.

Rhona had moved in right away, and she was glad that, by this stranger's kindness, she had been saved the return journey to Glasgow. Mrs. Rush had offered to send down her luggage and anything else she might need from the bungalow and had left, promising to plead ignorance of her whereabouts should she be asked.

As soon as the pram arrived, Rhona made up her mind to carry out Doctor Jordan's instructions, and take Robin to be introduced to his new medical adviser.

The doctor's residence was a big, white sandstone house with granite blocks at the doorway which glistened in the morning sunshine.

She passed the gate and then walked back and opened it, wheeling the pram into the drive. The house was hidden from view at this angle by closely placed rhododendron bushes which flanked the drive as it curved round the short lawn to the front door.

A door banged before Rhona emerged from the shade of the bushes, and crisp footsteps sounded ahead of her. She looked up and saw a woman in uniform coming towards her and then, suddenly, she found herself face to face with Nurse Brodie.

It seemed, for one blinding, panic-stricken moment that she was back at Kindarroch and had come in late from a walk with Robin.

Enid Brodie was frowning, but suddenly the frown gave place to a smile and she came forward.

"It *is* Grant, isn't it?" she asked quite pleasantly. "I thought you wouldn't be able to stick it at Kindarroch! Have you another place here?"

She had come close to the pram and now she was looking down at Robin. Rhona could not speak. She could only watch dumbly while consternation dawned in the nurse's eyes.

"Good heavens! are the Maillands here?" Enid asked at last. "It's the last place I would have expected to see *them*."

Rhona shook her head.

"It *is* Robin all right, Nurse," she said, "but—but he is here alone with me." Her mind was a blank when she ought to be thinking what to tell this woman, concocting some feasible story, but she could not think of anything to add to what she had already said other than the truth. Perhaps she could evade the issue by directing the conversation into another channel, she thought quickly. "Are you here on holiday, Nurse?" she asked.

"No, I'm working," Enid replied. "A friend in Edinburgh got me the job. It's quiet here, and the doctor finds me a great help now that he has lost his young assistant." She eyed Rhona speculatively. "Were you going in to see doctor?"

"Yes."

There was a short pause in which Rhona wondered if it might not be best to confide in Nurse Brodie right away. The particulars of Robin's accident and her own name would be set down in the doctor's case-book. Besides, what harm could it do? Enid Brodie was no friend of the Maillands and would probably never dream of divulging her secret.

Circumstance, that strange, silent player in the game of life, however, prevented the confession for the moment, as a large car drew up at the gate, and Enid Brodie said quickly:

"That's Mrs. Roystone. She has an appointment with doctor for eleven o'clock, so if you don't get in before her you'll be kept waiting for an eternity while she deafens him about her latest 'heart attack,' which is nothing more than another bout of indigestion! If you're here on holiday, I'll be seeing you. Good-bye for now!"

She walked on, a book under one arm, her medical bag swinging carelessly in the other hand.

Rhona stood for a moment where she had left her and then she walked quickly up to the front door and rang the bell.

When she thought of the interview afterwards she realised that she had gone through it like a person in a dream, the meeting with Enid Brodie dominating her thoughts while she made her halting explanation to the kindly faced man in the swivel-chair behind the massive mahogany desk and he examined Robin and told her that he thought he was well on the way to complete recovery.

The assurance was the answer to her prayer, yet she returned to the Camerons' cottage with a vague sense of uneasiness gnawing at her heart.

CHAPTER NINE

GERTRUDE MAILLAND stood at the window of the morning-room looking out at the fair lawns of Kindarroch stretching, dew-kissed, to the hills. Her fingers drummed impatiently on the back of a chair and she turned at the sound of the door opening with a dark frown creasing her brow.

"It's about time breakfast was served," she remarked to the elderly maid who came in with a laden tray.

"The second bell hasn't gone yet, Miss Gertrude," the woman said, laying some letters beside her mistress's plate.

Gertrude made no reply, but when Wilson had turned to the sideboard to attend to the coffee, she picked up her mother's mail and ran through the envelopes, scanning each address inquisitively. At the second last letter in the bundle she paused, the frown deepening on her brow, and then hastily she put the letters back in their place as Mrs. Mailland came into the room.

"Good-morning, Gertrude," her mother greeted her. "Isn't your father down yet?"

"I'm here, my dear," Hector Mailland remarked just behind her.

Mrs. Mailland sank into her chair.

"No word from Neil yet?" she asked.

Her husband shook his head.

"None."

The meal proceeded in silence until Gertrude broke it. She had barely touched her bacon and grilled sausage, and had crumbled a slice of dry toast into tiny fragments on her plate.

"Look here," she began aggressively, "I'm sick of all this nonsense about Alan's wife and her son and

179

having them back here at any price! If you knew how careless she had been you'd think twice and consider yourself well rid of her. She neglected that child to go running after Neil Murray and carried on a nice little side affair with Doctor Inglis into the bargain."

Her impassioned words dropped into a dead silence. Then, at last, her mother spoke, slowly, deliberately, weighing her words, it seemed, before she uttered them.

"You are quite wrong, Gertrude," she declared with absolute finality. "I've listened to this sort of thing from you before, but I've had a long talk with both Neil and Doctor Inglis and I find that our hasty suppositions were quite wrong. I've come to see—in a way—what that girl went through, and if Neil can find her for me I will try to make up to her for what has happened here. I can't understand why you still appear so vindictive——"

"Vindictive!" Gertrude cut her mother short by springing to her feet. "Vindictive!" she repeated. "That's rich, when you think of all I've lost through —that brat! But for him"—her voice rose until it was almost a scream—"but for him, Kindarroch would have been mine! Now do you understand why I hate them? Now do you see why I won't stay here one instant if you bring them back? You must choose between them—and me!"

Both Hector and Catherine Mailland stood looking at their daughter as if they were seeing her for the first time. In the old man's eyes there was a hint of hurt surprise; in his wife's, a deep and bitter resentment that any child of hers should have spoken thus.

"You seem to be upset, Gertrude," she remarked, trying to keep the indignation from her tone. "I can't understand you feeling that you have a right to Kindarroch when you realise that the child is Alan's son—a male heir in the direct descent. How *can*

180

you feel that you have been cheated in any way?"

Gertrude's cheeks were still flushed, the light of battle still in her eyes. Her mother's words seemed to have had little effect upon her, certainly not a calming effect.

"You weren't so pleased about the marriage at one time yourself," she reminded her parent hotly. "Wasn't it you who said that the girl who had 'trapped' Alan into marriage would never walk under our roof—or words to that effect?"

Mrs. Mailland moved restlessly.

"Yes, yes, Gertrude, probably I did at the time," she returned. "I was angry and bitter and disappointed, and I am not pretending even now that I don't think Alan could have made a better match— but it's all over and done with. He's dead, poor boy." Her voice caught a little and she coughed to cover her emotion—she who had so rarely shown emotion all through her life. "We must turn now to his son—to the legacy he left Kindarroch—and I feel that he expected us to welcome them both."

Gertrude bent over the table, leaning on her clenched hands, her breath coming swiftly—angrily —through her slightly parted lips.

"The day you welcome that girl back here," she declared again, "you say good-bye to me. That's final. I won't live under the same roof as her—with her baby smile and innocent ways that have snared you all—you and the old man and Jim Inglis and— Neil!" She straightened, staring at them compellingly. "I mean it," she added. "So you can change your mind or I clear out!"

She left the room without waiting for an answer and Catherine Mailland met her husband's eyes across the table at last.

"What are we to do?" she asked him for the first time in thirty years.

He answered nervously, hesitatingly:

"I'm sure I don't know, Catherine. Gertrude has always been a difficult child and she never seemed to have a governess who could lick her into shape."

"Her temper is most trying," her mother declared, frowning, "but I have no intention of sitting down under these sort of remarks. She will have to change her attitude."

"Then, you will not let this make any difference to our search for the boy and his mother?"

"Certainly not! Gertrude must learn that she is not mistress here." Mrs. Mailland let the suspicion of a sigh escape her. "Recently she has been most difficult in her attitude, almost attempting to take the reins out of my hands on more than one occasion. I have sometimes found myself wishing that she had an outside interest—some sort of work to do. . . ."

Her voice sank to a regretful murmur as she lifted her letters from the side of her plate and ran through them.

"Nothing from Neil so far," she remarked. "He's done such a lot for us and been so tireless in his endeavour." She looked up reflectively and across at her husband without appearing to see him very clearly. "Sometimes," she continued, "I wonder if, perhaps, he is just a little interested on his own account."

"I've had that idea for a long time," Hector Mailland observed quietly.

His wife roused herself to look at him more closely.

"Do you mean you have reason to believe Neil might want to—marry Rhona?"

He nodded.

"I wouldn't be at all surprised."

Catherine Mailland considered the matter frowningly for a moment and then her brow cleared.

"I don't suppose we could raise any objections." Secretly she felt a little doubtful about Rhona's return to Kindarroch, realising that there might be awkward little incidents to surmount, that first antipathy to be smothered and set aside. "However, we have no proof that the wind is blowing that way."

"If she married young Murray they'd want the child," her husband pointed out.

Catherine Mailland refused to consider this possibility at the moment.

"We're crossing bridges before we come to them," she said, and turned to her letters, her paper-knife slitting each envelope as if she were attacking an invisible enemy.

Hector Mailland lifted the morning paper, but he put it down again quickly at an exclamation from his wife.

"Oh!"

She was reading a letter and the thin pages fluttered in her hand.

"What's the matter, my dear? Not bad news, I hope?"

"Read it," she urged, handing over the flimsy sheets. "Read it for yourself."

He could see a dozen different emotions struggling uppermost in her eyes, rage, hurt pride, bewilderment——

The letter was written on two sheets of cheap notepaper, and began with the seemingly irrelevant statement:

"DEAR MADAM,—I am now in the A.T.S."

Hector Mailland found himself reading on in some surprise.

"I don't hold anything against you for dismissing me without a character, but I like justice, and I feel that it has not been done. I'm not caring for myself now, for I like my work here and it's fine and healthy, but I've been worried something

183

awful about Nurse Grant, wondering if she had been blamed as well as me for the accident to Master Robin."

Here Hector Mailland adjusted his spectacles to read on with added interest and a rising trepidation.

"Fair's fair, and I won't have Nurse Grant blamed for something Miss Mailland did herself. It was Miss Gertrude who sent me away from the nursery, and it was her who left the door open when she ran back to the garden, and I know for certain that she went down by the tower way. She did it on purpose so as to get someone into trouble, or get us all dismissed, and that's true fact.

"I'm sorry if I have worried you, but I had to get it all off my chest; and I hope the baby came to no harm and that Nurse Grant hasn't been dismissed through no fault of her own.

"Yours faithfully,
"AGNES HALLIDAY."

Hector Mailland sat staring at the somewhat involved ending to this amazing missive.

"This is rather serious, is it not, Catherine?" he commented.

"Serious!" His wife rose heavily to her feet. "If it's true, it is certainly serious, and I mean to sift the matter to the bottom."

She rang the bell at her elbow, but before the maid could answer her summons, Gertrude herself came into the room dressed in tweeds and pulling on a pair of fur-backed gloves.

Her mother handed her the letter in silence and she read it through and tossed it contemptuously on the table.

"Housemaid's twaddle!" she scoffed. "When did this come?"

"This morning. I want to hear what you have to say about it."

"I've nothing to say about it," Gertrude retorted, the flush of anger staining her pale cheeks immediately she was challenged. "If you choose to believe every lying housemaid you sack, well, I can't help it, can I?"

"I think you will admit Halliday received her notice before I returned from Inverness," her mother reminded her frigidly. "She was dismissed before I had any opportunity of questioning her."

Gertrude's eyes flashed.

"So, you accept her word, do you?" she cried. "Well, what of it? Suppose I did send her out of the nursery? She had no right to be there. It was Grant's job."

"Nurse Grant had been called downstairs—by *you*, Gertrude."

There was accusation in the older woman's voice and horror in her eyes.

Gertrude laughed.

"Are you accusing me of attempted murder?" she demanded boldly.

"That is a strong term, Gertrude," her father put in sternly. "We would not have used it."

"You may have thought it, though!" she cried. "Well, think it if you like! It didn't come off, anyway, so your precious name won't be dragged through the mud!" She laughed recklessly. "Yes, think what you like now! I've made up my mind to go in any case."

She turned to the door, but her mother had moved before her and barred her way.

"This wild talk must cease, Gertrude," she said firmly. "Where are you going?"

Her daughter faced her defiantly.

"I'm going to carry out a plan I've had for years," she informed her calmly. "I'm going to buy Lynne House back and go to live there. It's on the market."

Hector rose to his feet at the mention of the small property in the south of England which they had owned for some time and had sold a few years back.

"Don't interfere!" Gertrude advised before he could speak. "I've got the money to do it, so I'm not asking you for anything. I sold these shares you gave me at a big profit—Neil Murray did that for me—just in time," she added with a bitter little laugh.

She had gone before either of them could speak, and it was some time before Catherine Mailland said sadly:

"She was always crazed with the desire for possession—even as a child. Perhaps this is the only way she will find a measure of happiness."

CHAPTER TEN

RHONA had been at Inellen for two weeks and, though she had seen Enid Brodie at a distance, she had never come face to face with her former senior at Kindarroch.

Deep down in her heart, when she allowed herself to think of these things, was still that empty place which had once been filled by thoughts of Neil Murray and all he had come to stand for in her lonely life, but she believed that he had failed her, even that he had betrayed her.

So the days passed, with a deep grief hidden behind an ever-present joy, and she walked beside the sea with her child and thought of Neil in spite of herself.

Yet, she believed her heart hardened against him, and on the afternoon of a dull, wet day, when she saw him striding up the path leading to the cottage, she forced her trembling lips to a stern line and stood waiting to receive him. Somehow, she thought vaguely, she had known he would find her eventually, but she was ready. In the interval of two weeks she had changed, experience had hardened her.

Neil came into the room as if he had found some long-sought eldorado.

"Rhona!"

He stretched out his hands to her, but she drew back from him coldly.

"What have you come for? If you have come to take Robin you will find that I mean to fight you this time every step of the way!"

"My dear!" He came forward in spite of her hasty gesture which bade him keep his distance. "You must listen, Rhona, first——"

"Listen! Why should I listen to you? I know all there is to know!" Something seemed to have snapped within her and all the pent up agony of fear and pain welled in her heart, overflowing in a flood of words over which she had no control. "I know you gained my friendship only to turn it to your own use—the Maillands' use—a second time! I know you brought them to Giffnock, hunting me down because you saw it as your duty to—your clients!"

She flung the last word at him defiantly and was glad when she saw the hurt look in his eyes deepening to actual pain. He did not retreat, however, and suddenly he had discarded his stick and caught her by the arms, looking down at her intently, his mouth hard.

"You're quite wrong, you know, but that's beside the point," he said, dismissing the personal element with obvious reluctance. "I *have* come here on the Maillands' behalf, though not in the way you think. You must listen to what I have to say."

She strove to free herself, but his grip tightened.

"You must hear me, Rhona," he repeated almost

sharply. "Catherine and Hector Mailland want you back."

She tried to force a laugh.

"You mean, they want Robin, don't you?"

"They want you both."

She raised angry eyes to his.

"You can't trick me into parting with Robin again!" she cried.

He flinched before the accusation, but he did not release her.

"There was never any question of trickery," he told her, "though I can hardly expect you to believe that. Surely, Rhona," he appealed, "you can make allowance for a change of heart? Mrs. Mailland has acknowledged her mistake and the old man is wandering about disconsolately, waiting for my news."

"The news that you have won?"

He looked steadily into her defiant eyes.

"The news that I have not made a hash of their appeal," he told her.

Something of his earnestness seemed to pierce the hard shell of her resolve. She quivered a little in his hold, and instantly he set her free.

"Won't you consider it, Rhona? I can't bear to think of you here—among strangers—when you might have a home at Kindarroch."

The personal element in his confession was lost, smothered in another thought. Her eyes hardened again.

"I will never go back to Kindarroch as long as Gertrude is there. I—couldn't——" she added in a sudden, broken whisper that shattered her defiance and restored to him the woman he had always known.

He came over to her and laid his hands gently on her shoulders.

"Rhona," he said simply, "would you go to Dulmore?"

He saw her eyes change, all the hardness of despair going out of them to leave them deep wells of longing, and his pulses stirred madly. Then, slowly, she shook her head.

"How could I?"

He put his hand under her chin and forced her to meet his eyes.

"As my wife."

She stood for a moment irresolute and then she seemed to crumple in a little heap against him, but his arms were already round her, holding her close.

"What will they say?" she asked at last into the rough tweed of his coat.

"Does it matter very much?" He was caressing her hair with a hand that was not quite steady. "I don't think they'll be greatly surprised. Your father-in-law said as much just before I came here in search of you."

"How did you know I was here?" she asked, still clinging to him.

"Nurse Brodie wrote to Jim Inglis and mentioned that she had met you," he explained. "They're related, you know. Enid Brodie married a cousin of Jim's who died several years after their marriage."

"I always wondered what there was between them," Rhona said. "Gertrude flung it up at Nurse Brodie once or twice——"

She broke off, shivering a little at the thought of her sister-in-law.

"Neil—they can't part Robin and me, can they? They won't force me to let him stay at Kindarroch? Gertrude——"

He smiled down at her.

"Gertrude has left Kindarroch," he said, "and, as my wife, you will bring your son to Dulmore. The Maillands will have to be content with seeing him as often as they like until he comes of age. It isn't far across the loch!"

She turned her face up to him willingly, and their bargain was sealed by their first kiss.

THE END

To our devoted Harlequin Readers:
Fill in handy coupon below and send off this page.

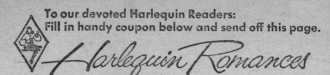

Harlequin Romances

TITLES STILL IN PRINT

51417 DOCTOR IN INDIA, P. Cumberland

51418 A CURE WITH KINDNESS, R. Clemence

51419 SO ENCHANTING AN ENEMY, M. Malcolm

51420 PRECIOUS WAIF, A. Hampson

51421 PARISIAN ADVENTURE, E. Ashton

51422 THE SOPHISTICATED URCHIN, R. Heneghan

51423 SULLIVAN'S REEF, A. Weale

51424 THE VENGEFUL HEART, R. Leigh

51425 GOOD MORNING, DOCTOR HOUSTON, L. Gillen

51426 GUARDIAN NURSE, J. Dingwell

51427 TO SING ME HOME, D. Smith

51428 NIGHT OF THE SINGING BIRDS, S. Barrie

51429 THE MAN IN POSSESSION, H. Pressley

51430 HUNTER'S MOON, H. Reid

51431 THE OTHER LINDING GIRL, M. Burchell

51432 TAKE THE FAR DREAM, J. Donnelly

〜〜〜〜〜〜〜〜〜〜〜〜〜〜〜〜〜〜〜

Harlequin Books, Dept. Z

Simon & Schuster, Inc., 11 West 39th St.
New York, N.Y. 10018

☐ Please send me information about Harlequin Romance Subscribers Club.

Send me titles checked above. I enclose .50 per copy plus .15 per book for postage and handling.

Name ....

Address ....

City .... State .... Zip ....

MAIL THIS COUPON TODAY